PHANTOM
HORSE
COMES HOME

Christine Pullein-Thompson

PHANTOM HORSE
COMES HOME

AWARD PUBLICATIONS LIMITED

ISBN 978-1-84135-822-2

Illustrated by Eric Rowe
Cover illustration by Jennifer Bell

This edition first published 2011

Published by Award Publications Limited,
The Old Riding School, The Welbeck Estate,
Worksop, Nottinghamshire, S80 3LR

www.awardpublications.co.uk

111

Printed in the United Kingdom

1

"Come in," called Mum, opening a window. "Something has happened."

I was schooling Phantom behind Mountain Farm. It was one of those lovely spring evenings which seem as though they would last for ever. The frogs were croaking incessantly in the valley and there was an exhilarating breeze which came straight from the Blue Ridge Mountains. I had been circling, and Phantom was beginning to flex his neck and drop his jaw at last.

I wondered what could have happened as I rode towards the stable which our American friends called the barn. My brother Angus appeared on a bicycle. He was having one of his non-riding days.

"What's happened?" he shouted.

"I don't know," I answered, dismounting and untacking Phantom.

I remembered that my parents had written to various hotels about a holiday. They had been torn between Cape Cod and a holiday in

Maine, which they said resembled England. We all yearned for England sometimes; when the days were unbearably hot or we were stuck in an endless traffic jam or people laughed at us because we walked to the local drugstore.

"They must have booked a holiday," I replied, walking towards the house.

"Yeah, sure," replied Angus, who was beginning to talk like an American.

Our parents were in the sitting-room. They each had a glass of sherry. Dad had just returned from Washington and was wearing an English suit. He looked tall and thin and on edge. Mum was looking out of a window.

"Oh, here you are," she said, turning round.

I took off my riding-hat. I felt nervous now. I wondered whether some close relation had died – there was that sort of atmosphere in the room.

"Well, what's happened?" asked Angus, throwing himself into a chair.

"Someone has died. Aunt Agatha, Uncle George, Granny?" I guessed.

Time seemed to be passing very slowly until Mum said, "You tell them," and looked at Dad.

"You may be pleased," he said unexpectedly. "We've got to go home."

"To England?" I asked stupidly.

"But why?" asked Angus. "I thought we were here for three years."

I thought of the narrow winding lanes, of Sparrow Cottage, small and dreaming, of the paddock where our ponies had grazed beneath the tall trees. We had only been in Virginia nine months, but already it seemed like years.

"What about school?" I asked, before I thought of Phantom and felt a lump rising in my throat. "What about Phantom?" I shouted. "I can't leave him behind."

"I don't know," replied Dad. "I don't know why you have to collect animals wherever you go."

I think I had better explain about Phantom. He is a palomino, golden dun with a flaxen mane and tail. He was wild in the mountains when we first came to Virginia. He had been destined for the racetrack, but he had broken loose and no one had been able to catch him. Angus and I and our American friends, Phil, Pete and Wendy, had tried and failed like everyone else. And whoever caught him could have him; we thought of little else during our first few weeks in Virginia. Then in the winter I had found him ill in the mountains, almost too weak to walk, and had led him down from the Blue Ridge Mountains to Mountain Farm. We nursed him back to health and then slowly I had tamed him, hung sacks of hay over his back, watched him shivering with fright beneath their weight, and finally ridden him.

"Can't you turn him loose again?" Mum asked. I shook my head.

"He causes too much trouble. Sooner or later someone would shoot him," I replied. "When are we going, anyway? He's entered for a show in May."

"In a month," Dad replied. "The government has changed – there's been an election. They want me in London. I've got to brief the new man and then stay on at the Foreign Office."

"It's a step up actually," Mum said.

"He was going in the green hunter class," I said, and my voice did not sound like my own any more. "The show is on the sixteenth. It was to be his debut."

"That's all right then," Dad answered. "We are going on the nineteenth."

"I don't know why you're so upset," Angus said. "I think it will be nice to see good old London again."

I had forgotten what London was like. I had become geared to the American way of life. I had not wanted to leave England a year ago, and now I did not want to leave Virginia.

"We get help with travelling expenses, so we might be able to take him," Mum said.

"You mean Phantom?" I cried.

"He would never load," Angus said. "He's too nervous. He would go berserk if he saw a ship."

8

"He would go by air," Dad replied. "But are you sure he's legally yours, Jean?"

I nodded. "His owner gave me a certificate of gift. He said I had sure earned him."

My mind was racing ahead all the time. I saw myself saying goodbye to Phil, Pete and Wendy. I might never see them again. I felt near to tears. "I don't know why things have to change," I cried angrily.

"That's life," replied Mum. "It wasn't meant to be a picnic."

"Supposing Phantom doesn't load?" asked Angus.

"They'll sedate him," Mum replied, "and tie him up so he can't hurt himself."

I saw Phantom being drugged, myself waiting for him at Heathrow airport, myself going back to my old school, meeting my old friends to whom I had said goodbye only last year. Our ponies would come back, grey Moonlight and roan Mermaid. They would graze again under our Oxfordshire trees.

"The fences won't be high enough," I said suddenly. "Phantom will jump them." I started to bite my nails, something I hadn't done for ages. The future seemed fraught with difficulties. "I won't have any suitable tack," I said. "Everything we have here belongs to the Millers."

"We must buy some tack then," replied Dad, sounding weary. "And build fences. It's lucky the cottage hasn't been let again yet. Things could be much worse."

"When shall we tell the Millers?" I asked next.

"Tomorrow – we can ride over in the morning, it's Saturday," replied Angus, getting out of the chair in which he had been sitting. "And for goodness sake cheer up; we're not all going to be painlessly destroyed. I'm looking forward to seeing Moonlight again, even if you don't care tuppence for Mermaid."

"Don't be so beastly. Of course I care about Mermaid," I answered.

"But you prefer Phantom," my brother retorted, leaving the room.

I could hardly sleep that night. There was bright moonlight outside, an owl hooted, and England seemed farther and farther away. I kept wondering whether Angus was right. Did I really like Phantom better than my thirteen-hand roan Mermaid? Then I started worrying about Phantom again – supposing all the planes were fully booked? Supposing no one could fit him in anywhere. What would I do then?

Mum came into my room on tiptoe and drew my curtains. "Do try and sleep, Jean," she said, tucking me in. "Everything will work out all right in the end."

"Are you sure?" I asked, grabbing her hand.

"Certain," she replied. "Dad will fix up

everything. He will pull all the right strings, as he always does." She brushed my face with her hand and went out.

I slept – and the next thing I knew was Angus shaking me, saying, "It's nearly ten o'clock, aren't you getting up at all? I've caught Phantom and Pelican."

Pelican was a wall-eyed grey lent to us by the Millers. He was a strange horse. He seemed to live removed from us all in his own private world. If you held out a titbit he just ignored it. Yet he was not blind, only wall-eyed. He never grew fat either. He was stiff and unresponsive to leg aids. He was fifteen-two, and sometimes we wondered how we would feel back on our own much smaller ponies in England.

I got out of bed and dressed in the inevitable jeans and bright checked shirt, which came from the one and only clothes shop in the nearest town. It was hot already; the frogs were croaking in the valley. The sun looked pitiless in the endless blue sky.

Phantom whinnied when he saw me. I tacked him up and we rode away across the valley towards the Millers' house, standing white and imposing in the distance.

"England is going to look awfully shut in after this," Angus said, pushing Pelican into a canter. It seemed as if you could canter for ever. It made you feel like a cowboy.

"Phil and Pete won't be there," I said.

"I know," Angus answered. "But we can still tell Wendy and her parents."

We had nearly reached the house now, with its white-railed garden which the Millers called a yard. Their white-faced, red cattle were standing half in the stream, shaking their heads against the flies. Their dogs got up and came over to greet us. It seemed impossible that we were leaving, going away, never coming back. Tears blinded me for a moment but Phantom walked on, his head high, his hoofs almost prancing over the nearly parched grass.

We found Wendy in the yard grooming her roan, Easter. "Hi," she called. "I was just going to ride over."

"We beat you to it then," replied Angus, dismounting.

They smiled at one another and suddenly I felt shut out, unnecessary.

"We are going," Angus said. "Dad has been recalled." He made it sound like a death-knell.

I dismounted and loosened Phantom's girth. Soon, I thought, all this will be just a memory.

"Going? Going back home? But I thought you – " cried Wendy.

"So did we," interrupted Angus. "But there's been an election."

"Oh heck!" shouted Wendy. "You can't go! We've made all sorts of plans. We've found you a place at Cape Cod for the summer." She had stopped grooming Easter. She was tall, far taller than me, with hazel eyes and red-brown hair which always seemed to stay where she wanted it. Like me, she was wearing the usual checked shirt and jeans. "Can't you stay on here? We can put you up. There's enough room in the old place for an army," she cried. "Your father must be coming back eventually."

Angus shook his head. "We've never been posted to the same place twice. Besides, he was due for a spell in England sooner or later."

"Of all the rotten luck!" exclaimed Wendy. "How about the show? You won't be gone by then, surely?"

I shook my head. "Not till the nineteenth," I replied.

"You could follow them later. Sure you could," Wendy said. "You don't have to go when they do."

"Yes we do," I replied. "And I shall be taking Phantom."

"He'll never load. You must be nuts if you think he'll load," Wendy cried. "Look at him; he's still half wild. Look at his eyes, Jean. He belongs here in the mountains."

"I'm taking him," I replied with a feeling of fury mounting inside me. "He's mine. I've got the deed of gift."

"I bet you fifty dollars he won't load," shouted Wendy.

"Done," I cried.

She looked hot and angry. She had wanted to dominate me from the moment we had met nine months ago. Suddenly I was glad to be leaving. I looked at the dry grass, at the dust rising where some cattle were stamping under a tree, and I imagined England damp and green, small and cosy in a way America could never be. I

14

imagined meeting friends again, drinking cider with them, sitting on the lawn at home.

"Let's ride. You girls always quarrel," said Angus in an annoying, grown-up voice. Wendy was too big for Easter but we rode as far as the gas line and down along the rocky bed of an old stream. It was hot even for April and I kept thinking of the long hot summer that we would never now see, and imagining Wendy and her brothers still riding along the tracks Indians had used in years gone by. Mr and Mrs Miller were out and we parted briefly at the cattle grid which led to the stables.

"You tell your parents you gotta stay, tell them about the house at Cape Cod. Tell them you don't want to go back to your silly little island yet," shouted Wendy. "Doggone it, you can't go. We've made a lot of plans."

"England isn't a silly little island," I shouted. "It's the most civilised place in the world." But she didn't listen, only waved and rode away towards the stables, looking large and American on Easter.

"Well, you did put your foot in it!" my brother exclaimed. "You said all the wrong things as usual."

"She wants her own way. She doesn't really care about us; it's her plans that matter." Suddenly I hated her and Angus, everybody. I pushed Phantom with my legs and we started to gallop, on and on across the limitless landscape. I shall make her keep her word, I thought, I shall demand fifty dollars, and I imagined Phantom walking behind me into a jet, the doors closing behind us, people watching, clapping, Wendy scowling, the sun shining on the airport, home the next stop.

2

The next day was Sunday but we didn't go to church. I schooled Phantom; I tried to teach him work on two tracks but I wasn't very successful. Wendy appeared in the afternoon.

"I've put this together for you. You'll need it for the green hunter class." She handed me an ancient double bridle as she dismounted from Easter. "It hasn't a lip strap; otherwise it's okay," she added.

Angus appeared. He was nearly as tall as Wendy and already his face was tanned by the sun.

"Have you asked about staying here?" Wendy asked. "Just till the fall. You can stay with us. I've fixed it."

We shook our heads. We liked the Millers but their ways were not really our ways.

"Then we're going to visit you in the summer vacation," cried Wendy. "We're coming over. Dad's booking right away."

I tried to imagine the Millers in England.

Would they stay with us? How would we entertain them? And what about the food? Would they appreciate bread and honey for tea? I fiddled with the straps of the double bridle, while my brother said, "Sure, that's great," sounding impossibly American.

I tried to imagine them on our ponies. I could not bear to think of Wendy on Phantom. She would lose her temper with him, jerk his mouth, terrify him for ever.

"If Sparrow Cottage can't take us, we can sure stay somewhere else," replied Wendy, sounding uncertain.

"Of course it will. You'll stay with us, that's settled," Angus replied.

They will bump their heads on the beams, I thought, and the spare room is tiny, and what if Mr and Mrs Miller want to stay as well?

I put the double bridle on Phantom but he still didn't look like a hunter. "I shan't win anything, he's too showy for a hunter," I said.

"Are you coming with us in the truck?" asked Wendy. "We'll have some room because the boys won't be back home in time."

I knew their truck. It was not like a horse box, instead it had rails along its sides and no top. The horse jumped into it off a loading ramp.

I shook my head. "Phantom might not load. It's only six miles. I'm hacking."

"Hacking?" shouted Wendy. "But no one hacks around here. You must be nuts."

I saw myself riding along a dirt road. "It will quieten him down for the show," I answered. "I'll allow lots of time. Mum will bring the grooming gear in the car."

"Pete will be mad when he knows," Wendy cried. "He'll be mad at me for not stopping you."

I took the double bridle off Phantom. The day was growing cooler and the flies had been replaced by midges.

"He'll never get into your truck," I said. "And supposing he tried to jump over the sides? You know how wild he is. If he escaped I might never catch him again."

"Have it your own way then," replied Wendy. "But you could get a horse box for yourself if our truck's so darned crabby."

Mum made us tea. Wendy drank hers with ice in it, and pineapple juice, out of a tall glass with a special long-handled spoon which she dug out of one of the drawers in the kitchen. She ate biscuits, which she called cookies. Suddenly the sky was dark outside and everything seemed ominously still.

"There's going to be a storm," she said. "I'm going before it starts."

Five minutes later she was galloping away across the valley and I was saying to my brother, "How are we going to put them up? Who will they ride? The're too big for Mermaid and Moonlight." And the future seemed full of worries again.

"We'll fix them up somehow. We can sleep in the summerhouse and they can have our rooms. Stop worrying, Jean. I'm looking forward to them coming."

"But what about the horses?" I asked.

"We needn't ride," Angus replied. "We can take them to London, to Oxford; it will be a lovely excuse for taking them places."

"But will our car be big enough? Supposing Dad buys an ordinary sort of English car?" I asked.

Suddenly the storm broke. There were great flashes of forked lightning which lit up the whole sky and the rain fell in huge drops, soaking everything in seconds. We ran for the house, hoping that Wendy had reached home in time, and I remembered that I had never thanked her for the double bridle.

We started to tell Mum about the Millers coming to stay and she said, "Don't let's start worrying about that yet. There's many a slip twixt cup and lip. We'll jump our fences when we come to them." And I wished that I was more like her, instead of edgy and inclined to bite my nails; "temperamental", Dad called it.

Mum had already started packing. There

were crates in the sitting-room and the furniture Mum and Dad had bought was packed in cardboard ready for shipping. I spent the evening cleaning the double bridle. Mum and Dad continued packing. Angus lay in the hammock on the lawn doing nothing at all, for the storm had ended and the sky was clear.

The next day Angus and I travelled with Wendy to school carrying a letter for the headmaster with us.

"It isn't fair," Angus said. "We only had four days off for Easter and we won't get four lovely months like you in the summer."

"That's just your tough luck," replied Wendy. "If you won't stay. If you must go back like kids with your parents."

I found that I couldn't attend at school any more; I kept imagining myself in England again. American history seemed irrelevant now and I had done the maths before at boarding school. I drew Sparrow Cottage in Art and the teacher said that it sure looked English and wasn't it cute, and weren't there roses round the door?

None of the trees were in blossom any more; spring had gone and the whole landscape seemed to be awaiting the full fury of summer.

"We'll sure miss you," Mrs Miller said, driving us home one day. "I don't know what Wendy will do without you."

"We're like bad pennies; we'll always turn up again," replied my brother.

"But when?" asked Mrs Miller. "We've only just got properly acquainted."

"Dad will ask to be posted back and then we'll return with him."

"We'll keep Mountain Farm for you then," said Mrs Miller, stopping outside our American home with a crunch of tyres.

The show was only four days away so I schooled Phantom all evening. He would lead off on either leg now, halt perfectly and rein back. I had never ridden in an American show before. Everyone will point at Phantom, I thought. They'll say, "Ain't that the horse which ran wild in the mountains all that time – Sam Smythe's horse? Doesn't he look great? Is that the little Britisher what caught him? Hasn't she got him going real good?"

And Phantom would go round the ring like a parade horse, not a hunter, but the most beautiful horse on show. And I would have done the impossible, caught the wild horse and schooled him, the horse which no one else could catch. And besides being a compliment to me it would be one for England, where I had learned everything I know about horses.

I groomed Phantom that evening until his tail was like cream silk and his coat gleamed like gold. I oiled his elegant two-coloured hoofs and

imagined myself riding him down the lane to
Sparrow Cottage, and suddenly I felt happier
than I had ever felt before.

The day of the show dawned fine. Angus was
not taking Pelican but he didn't seem to mind.

"I'm not a competing person," he said. "And
what would Pelican win anyway with his wall-
eye and inflexible neck?"

Wendy was riding her father's horse, a big
grey called Seashore.

The day was hot from the start and I knew
that by lunch-time every living thing would be
stationary in the valley, cows standing under the
trees, or in the stream, people in deckchairs or
hammocks, or working inside barns and houses.

No one but the competitors at the horse show would be riding by lunch-time.

I had cleaned my riding-clothes the evening before. I had nearly outgrown my jodhpurs, my boots pinched my toes, my hacking jacket was too short, but at least I had a hunting whip and, thanks to Wendy, the right bridle.

Phantom was still clean. I tacked him up and Mum said, "Are you sure you'll be all right? Don't do anything silly."

Dad had taken the car to Washington. Mum and Angus were to come later to the show with the Millers.

I pulled up my girth and mounted. My tummy had started to flutter. "It's straight all the way. I shall be all right. Don't worry," I replied, straightening my riding-hat.

"Touch wood," shouted Angus.

I picked up the double reins, slid my little fingers between them. I felt like a million dollars now and I was still happy with the sort of happiness which seems indestructible, but which is really as fragile as glass.

I waved as I rode out of the gate. Phantom walked with a long stride, his head high, his ears pricked. I leaned forward to pat his neck as I rode past rail fences and out on to a dirt road. Straightaway Phantom started to trot, his neck arched, his hoofs hardly seeming to touch the ground.

We must have trotted for a mile or more when I had the feeling that Phantom had been the same way before, many, many times, perhaps by moonlight when he was wild, enticing mares from their fields to keep him company in the mountains. I made him walk as a huge car hurtled by, leaving a trail of dust behind it. I felt him quiver and suddenly I thought that perhaps he'd never been ridden on a road before. I turned him on to the verge and we trotted, and I watched the lather growing under his bridle and his ears grow dark with sweat. I hope Mum remembers the grooming things, I thought, otherwise he'll look awful.

The day was growing hotter and there wasn't a cloud in the sky. I passed a wooden house. A man lay outside, swinging in a hammock hung from a mulberry tree. England will seem kind of foreign after this, I thought. There were high rail fences on each side of us and stables in the distance. Behind us the man had started to sing, and his deep, throaty voice seemed to belong to the countryside. I could hear a truck coming now, its engine drowning the man's voice, and even then I had no sense of impending disaster. It came nearer and I felt Phantom brace himself. I shortened my reins. "It's nothing, just a truck," I told him.

He started to jump in the air and the driver shouted, "Hi there! Get off the road. This ain't no place for horses, no sirree." He stopped the truck as Phantom went up on his hind legs. I leaned forward, grabbing his mane. I was afraid I would pull him over on top of me but he came down again on the grass verge. I could smell petrol fumes and the driver was still shouting. Then without warning we were on the bank at the side of the road and I knew with an awful certainty that Phantom was going to jump the rails.

They looked enormous, higher than anything I had ever jumped before, and I had lost my stirrups. He took off and I hit my face on his neck and I could taste blood on my lips. Then he was over and I was hurtling towards the ground, all my hopes gone.

I landed on my shoulder. As I scrambled to my feet I saw him galloping away in the distance. He cleared another fence, taking it in his stride. He's going back to the Blue Ridge Mountains, I thought, I shall never have him now, and a great wave of desolation swept over me. The truck had disappeared. I suddenly remembered Angus shouting "Touch wood", but I hadn't touched it. I was filled with superstition and regret.

I imagined Dad cancelling the booking for Phantom, the collecting ring steward at the show calling my name over and over again, men in white Panama hats turning to say to one

another, "I knew she would never make it. A girl is no match for that horse."

My eyes were pricking with tears. The heat was unbearable, the fields seemed endless and the Blue Ridge Mountains never seemed to grow any nearer. My boots were pinching my toes so I took them off and walked barefoot, keeping my eyes open for snakes.

The sun grew hotter and, as I climbed a wall, I wondered whether Mum had left for the show yet and what she would say when she found I had never arrived. Would she and Mrs Miller look for me along the dirt road? I turned back towards the road because I didn't want to walk round and round in circles for ever, climbing fence after fence and never getting any nearer home. It was even hotter on the road; nothing seemed to move besides myself. Small black pebbles got between my toes, so that in the end I was forced to put my boots on once more. Now I was hating the very size of America. I was thinking that in England the truck driver would have stopped, he would have helped me pursue Phantom. And then a truck did slow down and a voice called, "Hi there, do you want a lift? Hop in," and a young woman stopped beside me, holding open the cab door.

I climbed up gratefully. "I'm not supposed to take lifts, actually," I said.

"Where do you come from? You don't come

from here, I know that," she said, leaning across me to shut the door.

"England," I replied.

"And you've lost your horse," she said. "That's kinda tough. Are you all right, no cuts or anything? Did you hit your head?"

"No, I'm fine thanks," I answered.

She was young with fair hair and a white shirt and jeans and she drove her truck barefoot. We talked about England, and she told me she wanted to taste our fish and chips and I said, "You have to eat them in paper if you want to eat them properly." All the time I could feel my spirits sinking lower and lower and it was as though someone else was talking, not me at all.

"They sure sound fine anyway," she said agreeably.

We were nearly home now and I kept remembering how happily I had started out, without a trace of anxiety. I scanned the Blue Ridge Mountains for a galloping horse but there was nothing to be seen besides the trees reaching upwards towards the sky.

"This is where I live," I cried, pointing to Mountain Farm. "Thanks a million for the lift."

"That's okay, any time," she said. "I sure hope you find your horse."

"I won't," I answered, with a choke in my voice. "I don't suppose I shall ever see him again."

She opened the cab door and I stepped out into the heat of midday. My shirt was sticking to my back. My toes felt raw in my boots. She waved and smiled and waved again and shouted, "I'll be seeing you." And as she drove away I thought: That was one lift which was all right anyway.

I walked towards the house and as I walked I could feel the tears coming, first as a trickle and then as a flood and suddenly I was running, shouting, "Mum, are you home? I've lost Phantom. He's gone back to the mountains. I've lost him for ever." I wiped my face with the back of my hand, mixing dust with the tears, and I thought I never wanted to see the Millers again. I wished we were leaving tomorrow. Then I remembered the double bridle and I imagined Phantom hung up somewhere by the reins, struggling till his mouth bled, and everything had the quality of a nightmare, only I knew I wouldn't wake up, it would be there for ever.

I imagined the house empty before I reached it, the blinds pulled down in the sitting-room, the large grandfather clock noisily giving time away in the hall. Time! I thought. It must be two o'clock, time for the green hunter class. I shall never ride in an American show now, never. My tears fell unchecked like falling rain on the short paved path.

I heard Mum calling from the yard at the

back. "Jean, where are you? We've got him, we've got Phantom."

My brother came tearing round the corner of the house and stopped dead in his tracks. "So you've got here," he cried. "I was just going to organise a search party."

I ran round to the stable. Phantom was standing in his box, still blowing, his sides dark with sweat.

"We couldn't believe it when we heard hoofs. He came over the gate. It must be five foot. Are you all right, Jean?" Mum asked.

"He came home. He didn't go back to the mountains. He didn't want to," I shouted, and for a moment nothing else mattered.

Mummy had loosened his girth. Gradually his sides stopped going in and out like bellows. He raised his head and looked at me and I said, "Thank you for coming back," and then, "What's the time? Can I still get there in time?"

"It's just gone one," Angus replied, looking at his watch. "You might make it yet. I'll tack up Pelican and come with you. I'll ride on the outside, between you and the traffic."

"I'll get him ready while you change," I cried, running up the stirrups on Phantom's saddle, for miraculously they were still there. I put the reins under them and ran for Pelican's pelham and saddle.

Mum stood by saying, "You're horse mad,

31

both of you. Do be careful. I can't stand much more."

"I'll keep between you and the traffic," Angus repeated a moment later, mounting Pelican. "You must enter. It's your last chance."

"I wish I could follow you in the car," Mum said. "Are your girths tight? Put your hats on properly."

"We'll be all right," I yelled. "See you there."

We were riding away now. "Thanks a million," I said, smiling at Angus. "I thought I was never going to see Phantom again."

Angus looked small on Pelican. He rode in one hand. We cantered along a wide grass verge and people leaned out of cars to look at us.

"They think we're mad, riding along a road," Angus said. "I suppose horses always go by box or truck here."

"It's like walking," I replied. "Only nutcases walk."

"He must like us to come back," Angus said, looking at Phantom.

"I know. It was almost worth falling off to know that," I replied.

We clattered through a village which consisted only of a few houses and a drugstore. People ran to gates and windows to watch us.

"Look," shouted Angus. "There's the show. Look over there." He stood in his stirrups and pointed. I could see a ring fenced by a wooden rail fence. People were riding round it in groups. "It must be the family class," he said. "Was it before the green hunters?"

I couldn't remember and I realised with dismay that I had left my schedule on my dressing-table at home.

Phantom's bridle was filthy, his sides coated with dust. There wasn't a trace of hoof oil left on his hoofs.

"We had better walk," I said. "Phantom's soaked in sweat. Can you lend me a handkerchief? My face feels filthy."

I could hear the faint sound of music and wondered whether Pete and Phil had arrived home yet from their military academy. There were hundreds of cars parked by the ringside and we could hear an announcer calling out numbers. There were flags round the outside course hanging limply on their poles, and children looking like ants scuttling about with numbers tied to their backs. I felt unbearably tense now. There was a strange flutter in my tummy and my legs felt like jelly. I spat on Angus's handkerchief and rubbed my face. Phantom stopped to gaze at the scene below. He arched his neck and pranced.

"He looks like a million dollars. He must win a prize. Come on, let's hurry," cried Angus.

I could see the outside course properly now, high and solid. Phantom danced into the showground and I saw Mum waving and shouting. "I've got your number. Your class is next in Ring Two. They're halfway through the previous one."

Pete was waving too. "They've been calling for you," he shouted.

"Holy cow! What happened to you?" asked Wendy, appearing on Seashore who looked marvellous, his mane braided, his hoofs oiled.

"I can't go in like this," I said, halting Phantom. "Look at his mane and hoofs. He's filthy."

"I've brought some rubber bands," cried Mum, delving in her pockets. "I'll fix his mane."

"Where's some hoof oil?" shouted Pete.

"I'll get a rubber," yelled Angus.

Someone was fixing a number to my back. The band was playing a march. Angus was rubbing saddle soap into Phantom's bridle while he stood like a statue, sniffing the air.

"They're calling you again, you had better go," said Mum.

3

I rode down a sloping field past a party taking bottles of Californian wine from an estate wagon. Phantom started to prance and I heard a man say, "Sure, that's the wild horse. I would know him anywhere, and that's the little English girl who found him dying in the mountains. She's sure got some nerve, that girl."

Pete caught me up. He had changed out of his uniform into jeans and a denim shirt. "Gee, Phantom looks good," he exclaimed. "Keep your nerve. You're doing all right."

He had grown some more. He must have been five foot ten; but Phil was taller still, six foot plus and still growing. Pete had fair hair and brown eyes and his nose wasn't quite straight. Phil was as handsome as a film star, with dark hair and a long, lean body. All the girls turned to look at him as he passed. But I preferred Pete, who was less spoilt and kinder.

I could feel my heart beating against my side like a sledgehammer as I reached the ring.

"So you've shown up at last," said the collecting ring steward. "I sure hope the judge will have you now."

The band was still playing the same march. It made me think of musical poles at home, of cantering round and round the damp green English turf on Mermaid, while the riders and poles grew fewer and my friends yelled, "Gallop, Jean. Look, over there!" Suddenly I felt a long way from home and more alien than I had ever felt before. Phantom started to snort and the steward said, "Okay. You can go in now."

The green hunters were lined up in the centre of the ring. A judge was looking at their legs.

"Good luck," shouted Angus, his voice sounding very English amid the babble of American voices.

"Walk on," I told Phantom.

This was the great moment for which I had worked for months, to show everyone that I had tamed the wild horse of the Blue Ridge Mountains; but now Phantom was running backwards, gazing at the ring with frightened eyes.

"He thinks it's a corral," I shouted to Pete. "Can you lead him?"

"I'll try."

But he was on his hind legs now. A second later he came down again with a piercing snort, which made the horses in the ring raise their heads in alarm. His tail was kinked over his back and he started to do a sort of high school dance. I leaned down and stroked his neck. "It's all right, Phantom. It isn't a trap," I said. I could feel him relaxing as I spoke. Everything's going to be all right, I thought, he's going in.

Then, from somewhere behind me, I heard a man say, "Hi, you over there, give me my whip. That's no horse for a girl. He needs a man to master him." There was no time for the words to sink in. For a brief second I was speechless and then, as I collected my wits, the whip caught Phantom round his hind legs. He leaped forward six metres or more, and then we were galloping. I couldn't stop him, nothing on earth could stop him. It was like running away on an express train. Picnickers scattered; children ran; there was a tumult of shouting from behind, and nothing in front but fields and the Blue Ridge Mountains in the distance waiting to wrap us in their silence and calm. I knew how he felt . . . he could trust those mountains, they were like the four walls of home to him.

I pulled on the reins without avail. He cleared a wall without pausing, his tail streaming behind him like a flag. I wondered what Mum was thinking, what the crowds were saying, and how long it would now take to school Phantom to enter a ring and not turn wild at the first touch of the whip.

All the time that I was wrenching and pulling on the reins. I wasn't really frightened, for I knew he would stop in the end, that then I would get off him and lead him home. But I shall never be able to ride him properly in an American show now, I thought, and they'll go hatching slanderous stories about him long after I've returned to England. The mountains were looming larger now. I could see the trees on them, they were no longer just a blue smudge in the distance.

I don't know how many fences we cleared. I sat still, a passenger on the fastest little horse in Virginia, and then at last I saw the roof of

Mountain Farm. He's going home again, I thought. He really does like living with us. I hope he likes Sparrow Cottage as much; at least Englishmen keep their whips to themselves.

I could see a car parked in the yard and people waving. The sweat from Phantom's sides stung my legs through my jodhpurs. All my strength seemed gone. Phantom broke into a trot when he reached the yard. He raised his head and neighed for Pelican and it was like a trumpet call from a returning warrior. I slid to the ground, my legs almost buckling under me. It was the Millers' car I had seen. They came racing round the corner of the house. Mrs Miller had her hair, which was so like Wendy's, piled on the top of her head. She wore a denim skirt, canvas shoes and a blue silk blouse.

"Heavenly day!" she cried. "Are you all right, Jean? We thought he was heading straight for the mountains."

Mum was there too, looking small and frightened in her cotton skirt, shirt and sneakers, and Pete was smiling his broad, kind smile. Mr Miller stood behind them all, looking round and cuddly like a huge brown bear. "That horse will never go in a ring. He'll always be wild. You can't teach an old horse new tricks," he said.

"He isn't old," I cried. "He's only six. I shall ride him in English shows."

"I bet you five hundred dollars he won't go

in another darned ring all his life," shouted Mr Miller.

From far away I heard my own voice shout, "Done," and Mr Miller's reply:

"Her of all people. She's sure got courage, that one."

And I shouted back, as I walked limping to the stable, "I've already got a bet with Wendy about the aeroplane, she thinks I'll never get him in."

Pete helped me to take the tack off. "I sure hope you don't lose. Have you really got all that money, Jean?" he asked. "The old man likes his debts paid."

"Sure," I replied, with a shivery feeling down the back of my spine.

"I'll pay if you like," Pete answered.

"Pay?" I cried. "I'm not going to be the one who pays. I'm going to win."

"You thought that this afternoon," answered Pete. "I'll carry the saddle. You look kind of tired." I took off my boots and walked to the house barefoot.

"You looked like someone from another world flying across the landscape just now," Mum said. "Were you terrified?"

"Not really," I answered. "But why did that man hit Phantom? We would have been all right otherwise. He was going to go in. He was, honestly. I could feel it."

I saw Mr Miller laughing with disbelief and suddenly I hated him. "Where's Angus?" I asked, "What's the time? I'm starving."

"About four o'clock, I expect," Mum replied. "Angus is waiting at the show with Pelican. The Millers are bringing them both home in the truck."

"I'd better be going," Pete said. "The truck's waiting. Be seeing you, Jean."

I watched him go, kind, broad-shouldered Pete, across the dusty yard. Mrs Miller was hooting the car's horn.

"They are very kind. They brought me here at once, even though Wendy was just about to ride," Mum said.

"I would like to kill the man who hit Phantom," I cried. "I would really. Why did he do it? It was none of his business."

"You'll never have the chance to do anything," Mum answered, putting the kettle on. "Dad rang through from Washington. Phantom's flying from Kennedy airport, New York, in three days' time."

"Why New York?" I asked. "Am I going with him?" Suddenly everything was moving too fast. It was as though life had been speeded up by an invisible switch almost to breaking-point.

"That's the trouble," Mum replied. "They want a groom, someone older than you, who is used to flying with horses."

"But Phantom won't know him. He hates strangers. He won't load and supposing he goes mad on the plane? He knows me, can't you see that?" I cried.

"Dad will be home quite soon. You can talk to him," replied Mum wearily. "I've had enough for one day."

I wandered outside and could hear the sound of crickets already, though dusk had yet to come. The air was completely still. The heat of the sun was cooling at last. Already I was privately saying goodbye to everything, thinking if I couldn't fly with Phantom perhaps I should leave him behind in the valley he loves. And then I imagined him being chased again through the Blue Ridge Mountains, facing another winter alone with the tracks deep in snow, with icicles hanging from trees snapped in half by hurricanes. I imagined him alone for months on end, lonely and deserted. I imagined him coming down to Mountain Farm in search of me and I would be gone. Then I heard a hoot and saw that Dad was waiting for me to open the yard gate.

"Did Phantom go all right? Did you have any luck?" he called.

I shook my head. "Everything went wrong," I yelled. "Angus isn't home yet."

Dad left the car in front of the house. It was covered with fine dust.

"I've booked the flight. Phantom's got to fly from New York. It was the best I could do," he told me apologetically. He looked tall, slim and cosmopolitan.

"I've got to go with him," I said in a tight voice. "I can't just hand him over to someone. He hates Americans. He was brought up by an English groom. It was when he died that Phantom ran away. Something awful must have happened in-between."

"It's a nice story, particularly if you're English," replied Dad. "But are you sure it's true?"

I nodded. "It was an American who upset everything today. He doesn't like Pete near him either and no one could be nicer with horses than him."

"They may be able to find an English groom. I did mention you. I may be able to pull strings. But it's all very difficult," replied Dad, going indoors and closing the door after him, while I stood listening to a truck coming along the road, rattling in the way the Millers' truck did.

I opened the gate. Angus waved. He was holding Pelican and the horses looked sweet standing and looking over the sides. There was a loading ramp at the side of the yard and when we let the back down Pelican jumped on to it without any fuss.

"It's real nice to think you're still alive," Wendy said, smiling at me.

"Thanks a million," I replied.

"I jumped Pelican round the outsize course. He went like a bomb," Angus told me. "So nobody can call him a useless old nag ever again."

Wendy waved as the truck left the yard. "Be seeing you. We'll call you up," she shouted.

Angus had his arm round Pelican and suddenly I wished we could take him too. Life seemed unfair. I had Phantom, but Angus only had Moonlight who was thirteen-two and much too small.

We turned Pelican into the field with Phantom. We watched them roll as the sun was setting. "There's only three more days," I said.

"I know," replied Angus. "And England is going to feel awfully shut in after here."

"We'll get used to it," I replied.

"Dinner," Mum called, opening a window. "Hurry. We are going out."

"What, all of us?" Angus asked.

"No, just Dad and I. We've got to say goodbye to some people. Someone's got up a party for us. We've got to go to Washington," replied Mum, shutting the window.

"But what about us?" Angus asked when we were indoors.

"You'll be all right. You are quite old enough after all."

"And there's the telephone," I said. "Can you leave us a number?"

"Yes, of course, darling," Mum replied in an absent-minded way. "I don't want to go really, but it's too late to refuse now."

There was chicken and sweetcorn for dinner, and a lemon meringue pie. Afterwards Mum put on a long dress, earrings and gold sandals, and Dad put on a dinner-jacket. Angus and I stood around looking envious.

"Go to bed and don't worry, oh and here's the telephone number," Mum said, giving me a scrap of paper. "If you feel lonely, ring the Millers and have a chat."

"Lock up after us," Dad told us. "And keep the door locked. We're taking the back-door key."

"We'll watch TV," Angus replied. "Have a lovely time."

The moon had risen. It always seemed larger than an English moon, but then everything in the States seemed larger; it was just the vastness of the distances, the miles and miles between horizons.

We listened to the car starting up. "Come on, now for telly," Angus said.

We sat and watched, one programme followed another and we could not bear the thought of bed. "Supposing they crash on the way home?" I asked Angus. "What will happen to us?"

"Why should they?" he replied.

"I feel all creepy," I said a moment later.

"Let's go to bed," suggested Angus, but now we did not feel brave enough.

"I'm sure I can hear footsteps," I said presently. "Listen!"

"You are so nervy," grumbled Angus, but I saw that he had turned pale. "It's only just eleven."

"I can hear a truck," I said. "It's stopped in the yard."

"You're mad," my brother cried. "What's there to be afraid of anyway?"

"It's someone stealing Phantom," I cried. "They must have seen him at the show. We must do something."

I wished I was braver. I was shaking as though I had a fever and my teeth had started to chatter, and fear is infectious. In a few minutes Angus had it too.

"I'll get a knife," he said going into the kitchen.

And then his voice came back quite unlike his usual voice. "You're right; there is a truck in the yard. It's got the headlights on."

"It must be all right then. I don't know why we are frightened," I said. "Thieves wouldn't have their lights on."

We looked out of a window and saw three men.

"I'll check the doors and windows just to be

46

on the safe side," Angus said, brandishing the carving knife.

I remembered things I had read in the papers – murders, beatings, people being tied up, their mouths sealed with tape.

Then we heard a banging on the door and a voice called, "Open up please. We need a light."

"They're lying," Angus said. "It's a trick."

"Hi there, what's the matter? Are you on your own?" called another voice.

And I, like a fool, yelled, "Yes."

Angus kicked me and shouted "No", muttering "Fool" to me at the same time.

We went upstairs and opened a window and looked out. The moon was obscured by clouds but we could make out the three men. One of them shouted, "We've got a flat. Have you got a flashlight?"

Angus found a torch and threw it out of a window. The man caught it and as we watched them crossing the yard I started to wonder why we had been so frightened.

"They look a rough lot," Angus said, "Rough enough for anything."

We went back to the television, but we couldn't concentrate any more.

I thought how peaceful it would be in England, how the people would talk like us and we would understand them. Then the men came back and one of them shouted, "Hi there. We've put the light in the porch," and presently we heard their engine start.

"We won't tell the Millers about it," said Angus with a sheepish grin.

"It was only because we're tired," I said. "Normally we wouldn't have been scared."

"Normally Mum and Dad would be here," replied Angus.

The clock in the hall struck midnight. We could hear the frogs croaking in the valley as we dragged our weary legs upstairs to bed.

"Only two more days," said Angus.

"Yeah," I answered, too tired suddenly to worry any more.

4

I fell asleep as soon as my head touched the pillow. The next thing I knew was Mum standing beside my bed, while the first rosy light of dawn pierced the curtains. She was still in her evening dress but she had taken off her shoes. For a moment I thought I was dreaming.

"You are awake then?" she asked.

"Sort of . . ." I answered, rubbing sleep from my eyes. "Was the party all right? Some men came in a truck." I was still half under the bedclothes.

"The gate into the road was open," Mum said. "The horses seem to have gone. There are tyre marks all across the field to the yard gate."

I was sitting up now. "Oh no!" I cried. "You mean Phantom's gone?"

Suddenly Dad was there too, still wearing his dinner-jacket. "I'm afraid so, Jean," he said. "We've been on to the state police already, so don't panic."

"The men in the truck," I repeated. "They

must have come by the field." The gate from the field led on to the highway. "You may as well cancel Phantom's booking," I said. "We'll never see him again now, not alive. It just isn't possible. It's fate," I added. "It's been against me ever since we knew we were going home. What an awful end to an awful day." I was choking back tears now.

"It isn't the end of a day, it's a new day," cried Mum, drawing back my curtains. "Look, the sun is rising."

"I don't care about the sun," I cried, leaping out of bed.

Angus had appeared in a dressing-gown. He must have heard us talking for he asked, "How did they get out?"

"The men in the truck must have come across the field," I shouted. "Don't ask me why. I knew they were a disaster. Why didn't we think of looking at the gates?" I was pulling clothes over my pyjamas now – jeans and a sweatshirt – as I imagined Phantom colliding with a truck on the highway. "Pelican must have led the way out," I cried. "Phantom liked it here. He was happy. He could have jumped the fence any time but he didn't want to."

I rushed to the window and looked out. The valley was bathed in the rosy light of dawn. The moon was still in the sky, pale and soft, like something old and faded. Nothing moved outside, even the frogs had stopped croaking and the flies hadn't yet risen from the brambles. I could see cattle lying down near the stream.

He's gone, I thought. I shall never see him again. I always knew having him was too good to be true. Horses like him don't exist to be ridden like other horses. It was a fantasy that couldn't last. There seemed no point in searching the valley. We had no horses to scour the mountains; it was too early to telephone the Millers for help and Dad had contacted the state police. I felt inadequate and useless. Mum had made tea. We drank it in the kitchen.

"He'll come back," she said. "After all, he came back twice yesterday."

"They may have gone to the Millers," Angus suggested. "It's Pelican's home."

"Sometimes I wish you had never learned to ride," said Dad. "I have to be in Washington tomorrow at eleven, I mean this morning. I think I'm going to bed."

At that moment the telephone rang. "I'll get it," shouted Angus. "Somebody must have found them." As he disappeared towards the telephone I wondered why he was so optimistic.

"Perhaps it's the Millers," Mum said. "They may have been woken by hoofbeats."

We could hear Angus talking. He seemed to be taking down an address. Suddenly I was too frightened to listen. I had a terrifying sense of impending tragedy. I walked up and down the kitchen biting my nails.

"They seem to be on the highway," remarked Dad, who had changed into pyjamas.

"Oh no!" I said. "Anything but that."

Then Angus returned to the kitchen looking very pale. "There's a dead horse on Highway Thirteen. It's grey. It could be Pelican," he said in a dull voice. Suddenly he seemed very small. "What are we going to do?" he asked. "Pelican isn't even ours; he's the Millers'."

"What did the police say?" asked Dad.

"They want us to identify him," replied Angus with a choke in his voice. "He's on the verge."

There was a short silence before Dad said, "I had better change," and his voice sounded incredibly weary. He's got to be in Washington at eleven, I thought. He won't get any sleep.

Angus and I found shoes. We didn't speak for suddenly there seemed nothing left to say.

Mum changed out of her evening dress into slacks and a polo-necked jumper. There were dark shadows under her eyes. Morning had come now, a bright summer morning. We all climbed into the car. The yard gate was open. Angus passed Dad a scrap of paper.

"That's the location," he said, "as given me by the state cops." He sounded older, sadder and wiser.

I wondered what the Millers would say when they heard that Pelican was dead. They might not make a fuss, they might just say, "He was an old nag anyway. We never rode him till you came. He just stayed out with the work horses doing nothing," or they might start ranting and raving and calling us "Blah blah English, who couldn't keep gates shut", for they were as unpredictable as English weather.

Dad drove cautiously and presently we saw a car and cops standing in the highway and drew up into the side. One of the cops called, "Are you the owners? He's over there."

Angus was crying now and so was I. Covering my face with my hands I started to get out of the car, thinking: Phantom looks grey in the moonlight, like a phantom, and I was remembering the first time I had seen him galloping free and wild across the valley, and how I had wanted him and sought him since that moment almost to the point of madness.

"I'll go first," said Dad looking at me. "You stay here. Tell me how I can identify him."

"He had shoes. He was flea-bitten. He had a wall-eye," Angus answered.

I felt as though I was suffocating, choking to death.

"I'll come with you," Mum said.

"We're cowards," Angus told me. "Why don't we go?"

I couldn't answer. Tears were running like a river down my face. Then Dad came back. The state cop called, "Good morning, sir."

Dad started the engine. "It hadn't any shoes," he said. "It was a dark grey and quite young, I should think."

"Poor thing," I said, but I didn't stop crying. Everything seemed sad now, life, the morning, the fact that we were going to England, the poor dead horse.

"We had better go home and sleep," said Mum. "We're all at breaking-point."

It was six o'clock now; the valley was coming to life. We could hear a man singing on his way to work.

Dad parked the car outside the house. "Good grief, what a night!" he exclaimed.

We went into the house and Mum made toast and bacon and eggs. Then we returned to bed and slept the dreamless sleep of complete exhaustion. When I wakened Dad had already left for Washington. Mum was preparing lunch. There was the steady buzz of traffic on the highway and I could hear Angus talking on the telephone.

"The Millers haven't seen them," he said, coming into my room a moment later. "But they are coming straight over."

"You might have waited before you telephoned," I replied. "What's the time?"

"One o'clock."

My legs were stiff when I jumped out of bed and my head ached. I dressed and walked slowly downstairs.

"You look awful," Mum greeted me. "Do sit down. There's only a cold lunch. Angus has been on to the Millers."

"Yes, I know." I sat on a chair and stared out of the window at the stable where Phantom had been only yesterday, which now seemed a million years ago. If only we could put the clock back, I thought. If only we had gone out and helped the men with the truck we might have noticed the gate was open, but we were too feeble, too scared. How I hate myself.

"Come on, lunch," Mum said. "Sit down. Where's Angus?"

"I've just been on to the state cops again," Angus said appearing. "They've got nothing to report. We've got two days, Jean, so do cheer up. We'll find them yet."

"With broken legs," I answered, "on Highway Thirteen."

"If they were still on the highway the police would know," Mum replied. "Don't be an idiot, Jean."

"I wish we weren't going home," I answered. "There would be some hope then."

"We'll look for them this afternoon. We can walk," my brother replied. And then we heard hoofs coming across the yard outside. We rushed to the window. Pete and Wendy had arrived, riding Frances and the bay mare.

"Hi," shouted Wendy, "what're you doing?"

They dismounted as we joined them outside, their faces red from riding.

"Tough luck the horses going," Pete said.

Frances was rubbing her skewbald head on my shirt. I remembered the hours I had spent on her back in the past. We had shared a great deal together, good and bad.

"We reckoned you could do with these," Pete told us, tall and sun-tanned, his shoulders slouched. "We've gotta go to Washington, but we'll be back later."

"Here's Mum," cried Wendy. "Quick take the horses. We gotta go real fast. She didn't want us to come in the first place."

They were running across the yard now. We held their horses, shouting. "Thank you," wondering how we could ever repay them for their generosity.

"Some friends," muttered Angus.

"They could have been furious with us for losing Pelican," I answered.

They were waving out of the station wagon's windows, yelling, "Be seeing you." And I wondered where we would find such friends again.

Mrs Miller's face was set and angry. "You do that again," she shouted. "You darned rebels . . ."

Angus was patting the bay mare, who had never had a name. She was wiry and quick, a real cow pony people said, while Frances was a proper apache with a long head and a canter which seemed to last for ever.

"We may as well start looking straightaway," Angus said. "Here, hold the bay mare while I get the headcollars."

The day was hot now. The ponies hung their heads. There will be a breeze in the mountains, I thought, there always is.

"Shall we separate?" asked Angus, swinging on to his saddle. "They can't have got to the mountains without jumping half a dozen fences which Pelican could never manage."

"I'll go to the right then," I answered, turning Frances with one hand. "Be seeing you."

Our horses parted without argument. The sun was in my eyes. "See you in about an hour," shouted Angus.

I saw Mum waving. She shouted something which I didn't hear. There were white shacks in the distance along the highway, and a line of electric cables and a plane crossing the blue sky as lonely as a solitary bird. And gradually, as I rode, I could feel hope coming back. Two days seemed a long time when I divided it into hours. Anything could happen in that time. I started to sing as I cantered, my eyes searching for horses, my mind planning the future.

5

I kept within sight of the highway and to the right of the mountains. Angus was riding towards the town called Middlesburg. The plane had disappeared across the horizon. I saw some wild turkeys, longer legged than the English turkeys. A man seated on a tractor was crossing a distant field. Cars passed incessantly along the highway, gleaming in the sunshine. There were boulders scattered on the ground. The night seemed to have belonged to another time and place. My feeling of panic had gone. I felt one with Frances, welded to her in the way a horseman feels who has spent half his life on a horse. I belonged to the countryside, too, as the cars never could.

After ten minutes or more I drew rein and scanned the horizon. Frances dropped her head, stretching her neck and blowing. I couldn't see my brother any more. I pushed Frances into a canter again. The sun was full in my eyes now and, as the day grew hotter, I started to long for rain, for the soft English drizzle which falls so often at home. And then Frances stopped. She raised her head and neighed and from somewhere quite near an answering neigh came back. I wanted to cheer and I wished that Angus was with me as I pushed Frances forward, leaving the reins loose on her neck, already seeing myself leading Phantom home, while Pelican followed, across the sun-drenched valley to Mountain Farm.

I unwound the headcollar from round my neck while Frances trotted joyfully towards some boulders where I found Phantom. He was half on the ground, his coat dark with sweat, his forelegs caught to the elbow in a tangle of barbed wire. Beside him ran a stone wall which he must have jumped without seeing the pile of rusting wire on the landing side. Tetanus, I thought, as I leaped on to the ground and he raised his head and nickered as though he had known all along that I would come in the end. I kneeled beside him talking. "It's all right," I said, stroking his wet neck. "I'll get you free. Stay still, don't worry."

All the time I was forcing back the tears which were threatening to choke me. He rubbed his head on my shoulder and tried to stand; and I saw the blood on his legs and the flies feeding on it as he sank back again on to the dusty, churned up earth. I pulled at the wire. In places it was buried in weeds and part of it was stuck under one of his shoes. I stood up and saw that Pelican was grazing peacefully on the other side of the wall and that less than half a mile away the highway wound its way to Washington. I shall need wire cutters, I thought, and the vet and an anti-tetanus injection, and even that may be too late.

Suddenly I felt resolute and determined. "I'll be back," I said, standing up. "Stay still. I'm going to get you free." Then I was vaulting on to Frances, galloping as though my life depended on it towards the Millers' house in the distance. Time passed slowly. It was ages before the house grew any nearer, and now the terrors of the night and early morning had returned. I saw Phantom dying of tetanus, the vet saying, "There's no hope. I'll get the humane killer from my automobile," and myself leaving for home without him.

There was no one in the Millers' yard when I reached it. I rushed to the house and Annie, the cook, found me wire cutters. "You look real terrible!" she exclaimed. "What has happened?"

"I haven't got time to explain, but Phantom's hurt," I replied, and she understood.

"The horse that lived in the mountains. Sure, I know him," she said.

I had left Frances tied to the yard gate. She was still blowing as I vaulted on to her back again. She did not want to go now, and though I could understand her feelings I hit her with the ends of the reins and somehow we crossed the valley again, jumping a stream, avoiding the boulders by a miracle. Phantom seemed hardly to have moved but his legs had fresh blood on them. I worked frantically with the wire cutters and, because I hurried, I kept cutting unnecessary strands. Once Phantom tried to get up, pulling the strands tighter against his legs so that the barbs sank deeper into his flesh. I could have cried then. The flies were besieging us both now and I had to stop to wipe them off my face, wishing that Angus would appear and hold the wire for me while I cut it. The sun had moved so I knew that far more than an hour had passed since we parted, but at last the wire was cut away and I cried, "Up, Phantom, come on, up."

He tried three times before at last he was standing on all four legs, blowing through his nostrils as though he had been galloping. The wire had left deep cuts and punctures, a perfect breeding-ground for tetanus, and small pieces were still embedded in his flesh. He did not want to move. I shouted at him and hit him with the headcollar rope and then he lurched forward like an old person stiff in the joints.

"We're going home," I said. "Come on."

I decided to leave Pelican as he looked peaceful enough grazing. I walked slowly, dragging Phantom and Frances after me. He'll never make the plane, I thought. They won't accept him. He was limping on his near fore, and his off fore seemed little better. His sides were tucked up and his mane matted with sweat, earth and blood. Then he raised his head and stopped and I saw that Angus was galloping towards us waving and shouting, "Jolly good. Where's Pelican?"

I stopped and waited for him. The blood was drying on Phantom's legs, leaving a crust on the cuts.

Angus halted the bay mare. "What's the matter?" he shouted. "What's happened to Phantom?"

The bay mare was dripping sweat on to the dry earth and I thought how hard we had used the Millers' horses and felt guilty.

"He was caught up in wire," I yelled. "His legs are ruined. He'll never make a show horse now, and he'll probably get tetanus because it must be more than ten hours since he fell into the wire."

Angus had dismounted. He looked at Phantom and sighed. "Of all the rotten luck!"

"I must have broken a mirror," I told him, "I've had nothing but bad luck for days now. Pelican is just over there. We'll have to lead him back along the highway later. There's no other way out of the field."

It was almost as though someone else was speaking, someone more sensible and practical than myself.

"I'll go on ahead and telephone the vet," Angus said, remounting the bay mare. "Phantom looks awful and so do you."

I wanted to say, "Thanks a million," but the words stuck in my throat. I watched Angus gallop away leaving a cloud of dust behind him

and I started to hate the valley, the blistering
heat, the soulless procession of cars roaring
along the highway. Suddenly there seemed no
point in anything any more. I started to wish
that I had never set eyes on Phantom, had never
caught him. Then I looked at him and saw how
large his eye was, how wide his cheek. I saw his
matted mane, his tail which he still carried as
though on a parade ground, his neat hoofs,
covered with blood and dust and I cried, "I'm
going to get you home to England somehow. I
swear I am."

Presently I could see Angus coming back,
waving his arms and shouting, "The vet's coming right away. I told him about the possibility
of tetanus. He says there's no time to lose.
Can't you hurry?"

"I'm trying to," I replied, "but he can't walk
any faster. Can't you see he's lame?"

Angus dismounted from the bay mare. "Mum
says if he's really lame you'll have to leave him
behind," he told me. "There's only two more
days."

"As if I didn't know," I answered. I could see
Mountain Farm, looking tiny in the distance
with Mum standing at the yard gate waiting for
us. I was very hungry now and my toes were
raw again, so I took my boots off and walked
the rest of the way barefoot, though Angus did
his best to persuade me to ride.

The vet arrived before we did, parking his car in front of the stables. He was called Dr Beecher, because vets in America had "Doctor" in front of their names. He was small with dark hair and he had visited us once before when I had brought Phantom home sick from the mountains. It had been winter then.

Dr Beecher watched us limping home. "So it's that darned horse again," he said. "He looks a heck of a lot better than he did last year."

Angus was leading Frances now. "Why don't you ride?" he asked. "You look idiotic walking without shoes."

I shook my head. I could not explain how I felt. I think I wanted to share some of Phantom's pain.

Mum looked at my bare feet and said, "Oh, Jean . . ."

Dr Beecher bent down to look at Phantom's forelegs. He made a tut-tutting noise before he said, "Put him in the barn. I'll get my case."

The sun was moving towards the west. The air was full of midges. The stable needed mucking out. Dad was not home yet. I wondered what he would say when he saw Phantom.

"Hold fast, little horse," said Dr Beecher, returning with a syringe, wiping a patch on Phantom's neck with a piece of cotton wool. I spoke to Phantom as the needle went into his neck and he hardly moved, only braced himself and then relaxed as the needle came out again. "Now another one; penicillin this time," Dr Beecher said, "and I'll dress his legs next. He's made a real picnic of them."

Angus muttered, "Some picnic." Mum offered to fetch some water. I didn't feel like talking any more. I kept seeing a plane leaving without Phantom, and wondering who would be looking after him then, dressing his legs, feeding him . . . what would happen to him when I had to leave in two days time?

Mum was talking now. Dr Beecher was winding a dressing round one of Phantom's legs. Angus had turned Frances and the bay mare out into the field near the highway.

"Will he be all right to fly in two days' time?" Mum asked. "We've booked a flight for him from New York. We're going home."

Dr Beecher didn't say anything for what seemed like minutes, but which can't have been more than ten seconds, then he said, "He's going to be real stiff tomorrow, and there's still a chance of tetanus. I wouldn't give him a lot of chance," he replied. "Can't it be postponed?"

Mum started to explain and her voice seemed to go on and on for ever. Angus returned and I gave him the thumbs-down sign. Phantom's legs were bandaged now, so I fetched him a bucket of water and then a feed.

Dr Beecher got into his car. "I'll stop by tomorrow," he said. "But call me up if he gets any fresh symptoms." His tyres left marks in the dust of the drive. The frogs were croaking again and from somewhere came the lowing of a cow, on and on as though she had lost her calf.

"I don't know what we are going to do. You must be starved," Mum said. "And Dad will be home in a minute and I don't know what he'll say."

"It wasn't my fault," I replied, more from habit than anything else; because I knew whose fault it was didn't alter anything.

"I would like to murder those men who left the field gate open," my brother said.

Mum made tea. I sat with my head in my hands. "I can't leave him behind," I said.

"If he gets tetanus they'll put him down. There isn't a cure," Mum said. "Not a permanent one."

"Why not?" I cried. "People aren't put down when they get it."

"Dr Beecher says horses tend to get brainstorms afterwards and that can be very dangerous if you're riding them. He says it might be different if Phantom was a mare, because then you could raise a foal."

"I'm going to nurse him anyway," I cried. "I'm not going home till he can come too."

Mum pushed a mug of hot tea towards me. She looked very tired. I saw that the packing-cases had gone from the hall. Everything left in the house besides ourselves and our clothes and a couple of cases belonged to the Millers.

"You can't stay on," Mum said. "I won't let you. Anything could happen to you here on your own."

"Such as?" I asked.

But Mum was looking out of the window now. "Dad's home. He's looking at Phantom," she said.

I rushed outside. Dad was coming towards the back door. "For goodness sake, what's happened to that horse now?" he asked. He was carrying a dispatch case and had taken off his tie. He took a clean white handkerchief from the breast pocket of his jacket and mopped his face. "Why's he so lame? He doesn't know which leg to stand on," he asked.

"Come inside," replied Mum. "There's been another disaster."

"Not another!" exclaimed Dad. "I can't stand much more."

I followed them in. Angus looked grave. We went into the sitting-room, which seemed set for disaster with all our bits and pieces missing, dust collecting, the floor dirty, waiting for a final wash before we left. We all sat down, watching the midges outside, and I wondered why everything always seemed so still when the day was hottest.

"Did you have the vet? What did he say?" Dad asked, sipping the tea Mum had poured for him.

"He's coming again tomorrow."

"I shall have to put off the flight. He can't travel like that. He'll have to stay here. I'm sorry Jean, but that's life." Dad stood up, spilling tea, while I felt despair and a sick sort of rage growing inside me until I was forced to cry, "I'm not going home then. I'm not going without Phantom."

I don't know when I started to cry but when the tears came they were a relief, like the fall of rain after a hot, humid day. "I'm not going, I refuse absolutely," I cried. "I'm going to stay here and nurse him. I refuse to leave. I refuse." I don't know how many times I shouted "I refuse."

Finally Dad said, "Go to bed, and stay there, you obstinate child."

I stumbled upstairs through blinding tears to my small bedroom which looked out on the stable at the back. I couldn't see Phantom. I supposed he was lying down. I sat on my bed and contemplated my future and there seemed no way out of anything, just endless frustration and disappointment. I could hear my parents still talking downstairs. My room smelled empty already and I saw that my few books had gone, the drawers in my chest of drawers were almost devoid of clothes, the lampshade I had chosen one sunny day in Washington had been replaced by the tasselled one which had been there when we arrived.

There must be some way out I thought. Life can't be as awful as this. There must be a horse hospital somewhere where they could nurse Phantom and then send him home afterwards. He might not load, but there must be some way of loading difficult horses. Perhaps they are drugged and loaded by crane.

I went to the bathroom and washed my face. Then I walked softly downstairs and saw that my parents were drinking sherry in the garden.

"There must be a horse hospital somewhere," I said, walking towards them. "Couldn't Phantom go there and then be sent home?"

"At a hundred pounds a week or more," replied Dad bitterly. "We haven't that sort of money, can't you understand? We're not rich Americans," he added. "I wouldn't keep Phantom here week after week either, even if I had the money, which I haven't."

I looked at him and I knew that he was trapped too. We were all trapped by circumstances we could not escape.

"We feel awful too," Mum said.

It was very hot now; it was going to be hot all night. It was the sort of evening when you long for a swimming-pool of your own.

I went round to the stable and looked at Phantom. He was lying down, looking drowsy, with his forelegs bent neatly under him. I had rarely seen him lying down in the stable before. Then I saw that Frances was missing from the paddock. Oh no, I thought, not another catastrophe! I rushed to the tack room and her tack had gone too. She's been taken by Angus, I thought, but why on earth? And why not the bay mare? I rushed to the front of the house crying, "Have you see Angus? Frances has gone," and then I could have bitten my tongue off for speaking at all.

"Oh no," shouted Dad. "He hasn't gone too?

This is the end, the absolute end."

"He must have gone to the Millers," Mum answered. "I told him not to telephone. I didn't want them bothered, so rather than defy me, he's gone by horse."

"But why?" I cried. "Why did he go?" And then suddenly I knew. He had gone to seek their help. They would be home by now after their day in Washington.

"We can't let them help," said Dad, coming to the same conclusion. "We can't possibly accept any more help from them, we are too much in their debt already."

6

We waited a long time for Angus's return, but
he came at last, riding through the dusk leading
Pelican like a traveller of long ago coming
home. "I hope you weren't worried," he called.

Frances was tired. Her ears flopped dully
backwards and forwards as she trotted and I
could see her eyes looked sullen.

Dad was lying upstairs on his bed. Supper
was over. Angus dismounted. "I've brought Pelican, and the Millers will have us to stay," he
said, looking at Mum. "Everything is fixed up.
You can go home without us and we'll follow
later with Phantom." His face looked firm set in
the gathering darkness. He suddenly seemed
older as he led Frances towards the stables.

"But that will mean another cancellation,"
Mum said slowly. "We are spending a fortune
on cancellations. Dad's just cancelled Phantom's
booking, and who will see you off? And will
you be all right travelling on your own?"

"Of course!" I replied. "Don't fuss, Mum.

We are quite grown up now." I imagined the Millers seeing us off, New York growing smaller, and then hours later England, small and green at the other side of the Atlantic. "I shall miss you terribly," I told Mum. "I always do, but I can't leave Phantom behind."

Angus had joined us now. "They were marvellous," he said. "They really are true friends. Wendy is actually looking forward to having us. The only problem is school – we'll have left. What are we going to do?"

"Stay away," I replied.

"We will have to discuss it with Dad," Mum replied, "Everything has been changed so often that I feel as though I was in the maze at Hampton Court. I don't know how we can go home without you. As for school, you're probably going to the new comprehensive school; it's very modern, and I don't think a few days away will make much difference as to what subjects you study."

"Why didn't you tell us before?" I asked. "I thought we were going back to our dreary boarding schools."

"It was only decided a few days ago," Mum replied. "Do come inside now; it's terribly late, and I've got to clean the house tomorrow."

"We'll help," Angus said. "I'm great at washing floors."

"I'll polish the furniture and clean all the

windows," I added, wondering what the new comprehensive school would be like; whether I would quarrel with Wendy, where I would sleep.

"We'll see you off," Angus told Mum, "then we'll catch the coach back here; it stops at the corner. I've discussed everything with Wendy." He was lit up by excitement, he couldn't stop talking; even when he was in bed he kept shouting from across the passage. "What do you think Dad will say?" he asked, and then, "You're not to quarrel with Wendy and we've both got to help, make our beds, you know what I mean."

"I always do make my bed," I answered. "It's you who doesn't."

"Phantom's going to have the best box. They are sending the truck for him as soon as he's better."

"When he's better we are going home," I replied. "By the first available plane."

I was almost asleep, but Angus's voice went on and on. Occasionally he called, "Are you listening?" and I managed a sleepy "Yes" but I wasn't; I was seeing myself entering a classroom with plate glass windows, smiling at the other pupils, trying to be interested in English history again. Then my mind switched to the journey home. Would we both be allowed to travel on the plane with Phantom? The future seemed full of frightful difficulties. Downstairs the clock in the hall struck twelve and then mercifully I slept.

The next morning dawned heavy with the promise of thunder. Phantom was standing up in his box, his forelegs swollen to the elbow. With shaking heart I looked for symptoms of tetanus but he could move his head easily and his neck wasn't stiff.

"I don't think he's got it," I cried, charging into the kitchen. "His legs are awful but he isn't stiff otherwise and he's eating."

Dad was spooning marmalade on to toast in a very English manner. "So you plan to stay with the Millers now?" he asked. "You're not coming with us?"

"I can't think of anything else to do," I replied.

"I wash my hands of you then," Dad said. "If that darned horse matters more than returning with us, stay here as long as you like."

I knew he was tired. I didn't know what to say and then, without warning, he started to laugh. "Oh, it doesn't matter," he cried. "It will give your mother and me a chance to have a few days alone together." And I started to laugh as well with a sense of relief.

Angus and I spent the morning washing the floors and helping our parents pack. They were leaving next day late in the afternoon, handing the car to a dealer in Washington, taking a taxi to the airport. I didn't want them to go now.

I had stayed with the Millers before when Angus fell off in the mountains and went to hospital. Annie did all the cooking and much else besides; and breakfast was a gracious cooked meal eaten in the dining-room.

At two o'clock Dr Beecher called again. "How is he?" he asked. "No tetanus?"

We shook our heads and took him to the stable. He knelt in the straw. "They're darned swelled, aren't they?" he asked, feeling Phantom's legs. "Will he move?"

"Not much," I said.

"He'll be okay in a week, I guess," Dr Beecher told us. "Try not to worry. He'll be marked, but he'll be sound and you can take him back home and hunt him. I'll come and check him again in a couple of days."

"He won't be here after tomorrow," I said. "We're moving him to the Millers' place."

"Okay, I'll call there the day after tomorrow then to cut off the dressings." He got into his car and drove away.

"That's another sixty dollars gone west," my brother said.

"Are you sure it's as much as that?"

"I expect so. Even an injection of penicillin costs more than twenty dollars," he replied.

I started to groom Phantom. His coat shone

like pale gold, his skin rippled under the body brush. It was three o'clock already, soon our parents would be gone. Phantom walked round his box slowly and painfully, like an old man on sticks. I filled his water bucket and a haynet.

"We had better go inside and help some more. Mum is getting into one of her panics," Angus said.

We ate a high tea in the kitchen. Our parents were dressed ready for their plane. "Aren't you going to change?" Mum asked, looking at our jeans.

"We're good enough for the Greyhound bus," Angus replied.

"But not for the taxi," Mum said.

I put on a cotton skirt, checked blouse and moccasins. Angus put on shorts and a sweat-shirt. Our clothes were packed ready to be dropped at the Millers' when we picked up Wendy in half an hour's time. I was feeling sick with apprehension. Supposing Mum and Dad crash? I thought. Who will we live with then? It was too awful to contemplate – even Phantom was not worth such catastrophe.

Our parents were both in suits. Mum wore a linen one with a frilly blouse underneath. She looked beautiful. Suddenly it was as though I was seeing her for the first time, as an ordinary person, instead of as my mother. We helped carry the cases to the car. Dad locked up

Mountain Farm. He walked towards the car without looking back.

Mum said, "It was nice while it lasted. I'm glad we came, anyway."

Wendy kept us waiting. She appeared at last out of the front door in a dress with buckles at the shoulders.

It was very hot all the way to Washington. I spent the time wishing Wendy had not come. There were lots of things I wanted to say to Mum but not in front of Wendy and I felt angry with Angus for asking her. Mum and Dad talked about shopping on their way home from Heathrow airport. It made me feel homesick. I imagined them walking into English shops, buying English food, English greens, cauliflowers, new potatoes. Wendy and Angus made jokes. Time was passing quickly.

Mum started to tell us what not to do. "Don't ride without hats," she said. "Don't ride alone. Don't take lifts from strange men. Help with the washing-up. Make your beds. Be polite . . ."

We were over the Potomac river now. We could see the Pentagon laid out like a model city. "This is where we leave the car," said Dad a moment later.

I wasn't going to cry, not in front of Wendy. Angus was still laughing.

Dad gave Angus and me most of the money in his wallet. "That's to last you till you get home, so don't spend it all at once," he said, hailing a cab.

"Where to?" asked the driver.

"To the airport," Dad answered.

"Give us a ring when Mr Miller has booked your flight home," Mum told us as we sped through Washington. "We'll send a horse box to meet you. I expect it will be Mr Price."

I nodded. It seemed impossible that we would ever reach England with Phantom.

The airport was full of people carrying bags. Dad went to check the departures and came back saying, "Our flight is leaving an hour late.

There's no point in your staying. Let's go and find a cab for you three."

"It only means prolonging the agony," Mum agreed, kissing me quickly on the cheek before turning to do the same to Angus.

Dad found us a cab. None of us felt like speaking now, though Wendy tried a few jokes in an effort to cheer us. "Be good," Mum said as we climbed into the taxi.

"To the Greyhound station," Dad told the driver. "Be seeing you."

They stood waving, looking heart-breakingly familiar, and for one awful moment I thought: Even Phantom isn't worth this. Then Wendy slapped my shoulder. "Don't look so darned sad," she cried. "You'll be seeing them again in no time."

"If they don't crash into the Atlantic," I replied.

"You're nuts," Wendy replied. "Planes are going backwards and forwards all day long. Didn't you know? Folks wouldn't fly in them if they crashed into the sea."

We had a half-hour wait at the bus station. We sat on a bench watching people leaving for far-away places.

"I wonder if I shall ever see Miami," Angus sighed. "Or Los Angeles, or San Francisco."

"Or the Rockies," I added, imagining myself riding Phantom through a mountain pass.

Wendy made friends with a boy wearing trainers, shorts and a white sweatshirt with the name of a club on it.

She said he was cute, and they exchanged addresses, sitting with their heads very close together, while I sat wondering whether Phantom had emptied his water bucket yet.

When the bus arrived, we bagged a seat in the front. Wendy was still talking about the boy she had met, and Angus had become gloomy and rather cross.

"This bus should have left five minutes ago," he said. "Why are they always late?" But eventually we reached Virginia, which was full of the smell of boxwood and new mown hay and lit by the evening sun.

We climbed out of the bus at the top of the Millers' drive. I turned left towards Mountain Farm, while Angus and Wendy started to walk down the drive towards the Millers' house, grumbling because there was no one to meet them.

I was pleased to be walking on my own across the valley. It gave me time to contemplate the future. Phantom greeted me with a whinny. He still had food and water and, miraculously, his forelegs had started to go down. I kept my eyes averted from the house. I mucked him out and fed him, tacked up Frances and rode away across the valley and suddenly I wasn't missing my parents at all; I was filled with a great sense of happiness. This is life, I thought. I'm living. I'm five thousand miles from home and in a few days I shall be flying with Phantom and Angus, miles and miles above the sea. Suddenly all my dreams seemed possible. My future seemed as boundless as the universe.

7

The Millers were waiting dinner for me. I turned Frances into the orchard beyond the stable yard. Their dogs greeted me, running round in circles and yapping. I found Annie dishing up in the kitchen.

"Do you like ice cream?" she asked. "Mrs Miller says I make it real good, so I made it especially for you."

"I love it. Thank you very much," I replied.

"Am I terribly late?"

She shook her head. "Dinner's just going in now," she answered.

We ate in the large dining-room, the table decorated with silver candlesticks with candles which weren't lit. Angus had washed his hands and combed his hair. He sat opposite Wendy, cracking jokes, making everyone laugh. I wished that Pete was with us. Mr Miller asked me about Phantom and I told him how he had improved already. The evening sun shone through the Georgian windows and suddenly everything seemed dated, old-fashioned, as though we had moved into some earlier age.

After dinner Wendy and I played the piano in the large drawing-room which was hardly ever used. Angus talked to Mr and Mrs Miller in the library, which had leather-covered armchairs and a shelf full of books about riding. It was all very pleasant but seemed far removed from home and Sparrow Cottage.

"Mum and Dad must be still flying," I said presently. "Isn't it amazing?"

I shared Wendy's room, which had windows with bright checked curtains on both sides, white furniture, and whitewood beds with checked covers. Angus was sleeping in the spare room, which was above the drawing-room and had a white carpet and a magnificent white and gold bed. It wasn't his sort of room, not a room for jeans and trainers at all.

Wendy and I talked for hours. She told me all about a boy she had known last year. He had written her long letters. "He was the best boyfriend I ever had," she said. "I guess your brother is all right and he's real cute, but he's kinda backward, isn't he?"

I agreed. "We're all kinda backward back home," I said with a laugh. "It's something to do with the weather and being so shut in." Wendy took me seriously, while I was laughing inside all the time.

"Yeah, it must make a difference," she said. "All that rain . . ."

I slept at last and didn't dream.

The sun was streaming into the room when I woke up and I thought straightaway: They'll be home. They'll be stepping out of a car, unlocking the front door, and the trees will be in blossom. And I wished I was there too, standing in the soft English air with the trees all pink with blossom and the banks still yellow with the last of the primroses.

Wendy was still asleep, her red-brown hair spread across her pillow.

I got up and dressed and found Annie making waffles in the kitchen.

"You want yours now? You want to get out real quick?" she asked. I nodded, wondering how she understood.

I sat down at the plain wood table and she gave me a plate of waffles, crisp fried bacon and maple syrup.

"You wanta see your little horse?" she said.

Later I tacked up Frances and rode across the valley to Mountain Farm. Phantom had upset his water bucket and the house looked deserted, as though it knew already that we would never be back. The hammock swung empty on the lawn. The doors were locked and bolted. "I'm taking you over to the Millers' place," I told Phantom.

I led him out, and he tottered for a time. He's never going to be sound again, I thought, and my heart seemed to be beating twice as fast. Then the stiffness wore off and he looked almost sound as I rode Frances and led him across the valley. I didn't look back at Mountain Farm because its very emptiness seemed to reproach me, as though somehow it was all my fault.

Angus was waiting on the lawn in front of the house. "You might have waited. I wanted to come too. What about Pelican?" he shouted.

"I couldn't wait," I answered. "I had to see to Phantom. He had kicked over his water bucket. Where's Wendy?"

"Getting up," Angus replied.

The Millers' stables were like old-fashioned English ones with wood partitions and doors with bars. But the wood was not varnished and the bars were unpainted and the floors were beaten earth instead of brick. I put Phantom into one of them and he stood by the window at the back of the box trying to see out. I untacked Frances and put her back in the orchard. Beyond the orchard the last of the hay was being carted. Inside I found Wendy dressed for school.

"Of all the crabby arrangements," she said. "Why should I go while you stay home?"

Mrs Miller drove her to school in her car

with the hood down. Angus and I sat in the sun chewing grass and talking. Time hardly seemed to be passing. Peace seemed absolute; there was no point in doing anything.

"Phantom will be all right to fly in a couple of days," I said. "Are we going to make the arrangements?"

"No, Mr Miller is going to do it," replied Angus.

"You'll have to tell him."

"I wonder where Mum is."

"Shopping, I expect."

We took our shoes off and lay on our backs staring up into the sky.

"I shall miss this," Angus said.

"Same here. One sort of expects the sun all the time here," I answered.

"We'll be wearing pullovers again," Angus said, "and riding-coats, and there won't be scorching central heating."

"But we'll be free," I answered. "We won't feel like poor relations any more." I stood up. "We'll be in our own country. It will be our turn to show people around for a change."

I walked to the stables and groomed Phantom. The boxes were mucked out straight on to a midden outside. Sometimes the midden reached nearly to the stable door, which the Millers always shut at night, so in summer, unless the windows were open, the boxes were stiflingly hot. Wendy insisted that the floors were good for the horses' legs. "Much better than your crabby concrete ones," she would say.

I gave Phantom some maize still on the cob and filled his rack with hay. I fetched him water and wandered up to the house, and it still wasn't lunch-time. Angus was lying in a hammock reading, Mrs Miller had gone to the bank. There seemed all the time in the world.

"I wish Mr Miller was here. I want to get everything fixed up," I said.

"Dr Beecher has to give the okay. What's the matter?" asked Angus. "Why don't you read or something?"

"There's nothing to read," I replied. "All the horsy books here are out of date. They're full of people with old-fashioned hunting seats and diagrams of bearing reins."

"Can't you read anything but horsy books?" asked Angus.

"Not at the moment," I replied. Then, "Supposing Phantom doesn't load," I said, "what shall I do with him? It will be worse without Mum and Dad. I mean Dad can always get round people, but Mr Miller will probably say, 'He's nutty, Jean, he'll never make good, not that darned horse, better put a bullet through his head.'" As I spoke I saw Phantom's beautiful head in my mind's eye and started to sniff.

Angus put down his book. "For goodness

sake," he replied. "Stop fretting. I've told you, they'll sedate him, so what the heck?"

"You're talking American, not English at all, do you realise that?" I asked. "People will call you Yankee when you get home."

I was being irritating on purpose and suddenly I knew why; there was another storm blowing up. The air was heavy and humid. The cattle were leaving the valley for the shelter of the mountains. I wandered inside and watched Annie making rolls for lunch. She was singing softly and she kept smiling at me as she worked.

The storm broke while we were having lunch. Mr Miller was still out.

"I guess it's a bit dull without the boys and Wendy, but she'll be back soon," Mrs Miller said.

Angus was in one of his chatty moods. He talked all through lunch, making Mrs Miller laugh, while the rain fell in drops as big as hailstones, drenching the valley in seconds.

Wendy returned from school later. "Gee, it just ain't fair," she shouted crossly. "Why should you stay home while I work myself nutty in that crabby school?"

Mr Miller was home by this time and we all wandered round to the stables together to look at Phantom.

"A call came through from your parents a

few minutes ago," Mr Miller told us. "They're home and send their love."

"Good," said Angus.

I imagined them sitting in our tiny hall and phoning while, as likely as not, rain fell through the trees outside. I wished I had been the one to answer the phone.

Mr Miller wanted to cut away Phantom's bandages, but we persuaded him to leave them until tomorrow when Dr Beecher would be visiting.

"He looks okay, Jean," he said. "I'll book you on a plane next week. What's today?"

"Thursday," I answered, after a pause for reflection, for the days had become muddled and, in some strange way, pointless now.

"Monday then," said Mr Miller, slamming the loose box door shut. "He'll be fit enough then and I'll sure be glad to see the back of him. Yes indeed, the trouble that horse has caused."

"If he loads," Wendy replied.

"He'll load. They'll see to that, else it will be the humane killer," replied Mr Miller. "We sure don't want him roaming the mountains again."

There was a red sun going down in a glorious pool of colour beyond Mountain Farm. The sky was red, gold and blue, the grass sparkling with raindrops.

"You sure won't see anything like this in

England," Wendy said. I nodded in agreement.

Annie was waiting for us with dinner on the table. There were gleaming glasses and starched napkins in silver rings. The table was polished until you could see your face in it. The old mahogany chairs had seats covered with striped brocade.

The Millers are going to find Sparrow Cottage very small after this, I thought. Phil will hit his head on the beams and the chair in the hall will break under Mr Miller's weight. But it will be lovely having them all the same. I will be able to show Wendy my books and Mermaid's rosettes, and, if they come in September, the apples will be ripe. I saw myself taking them to the village shop; old Mrs Pratt peering at them through her spectacles, saying, "You're not from these parts," in her quavery, cracked voice.

The next day Angus and I rode up to the mountains. We crossed the gas line and stood at Signal Post where George Washington was supposed to have stood, and we stared into the distance seeing the Potomac river running like a thread through the landscape.

"Do you remember seeing all this for the first time?" Angus asked. "I've grown kinda fond of it, haven't you?"

"Yes," I said, "I want to remember every bit of it for ever, even the smell, but I don't suppose I will. But one day I shall come back."

"Same here," said Angus, picking up his reins again.

We rode down to find Dr Beecher waiting for us in the yard.

"I've seen the little horse," he told us as we dismounted. "He's sure made a wonderful recovery. I should give him another day or two before you take him back home. I've given him another shot of penicillin, he'll be okay now. Put him out in the orchard this evening."

"Thank you very much. Can he go without his bandages?" I asked.

"Sure. Just one other problem. What about the account?"

"The account?" I said stupidly.

"Sure, here it is. I thought you'd like it before you go back home."

I opened the envelope Dr Beecher gave me. Inside I read: *Two visits. Four injections, two hundred dollars*, only it wasn't written quite like that.

"Yes," I said, "yes, of course," while my mind took in two hundred dollars and reeled at the thought.

Angus looked over my shoulder and nudged me. "We've got some money inside," he said. "Hang on."

We paid Dr Beecher all we had and watched him drive away. "Wow, what a price!" I said. "We haven't a penny for the journey now. And we still owe him money."

"Exactly, that darned horse, he'll be the ruin of us." Angus was laughing. "Who cares anyway?" he asked. "We'll manage."

I wished I was more like him then, instead of always seeing ahead, working things out before I reached them, perpetually fearing the worst. Mum says you're born one way or the other, but I think it's more an attitude of mind and if you can train anything you ought to be able to train your own mind.

I couldn't hold Phantom when I led him into the yard in the evening. He stood on his hind legs, snatching the headcollar rope from my hands, and careered away across the yard.

"Fool!" shouted Angus. "Idiot! Why didn't you hold on?"

"I couldn't," I shouted. "I tried."

Phantom tore round the yard in a mad frolic. Then he cleared the gate into the orchard in one quick leap and settled down to eat. I sighed with relief. "If only we can keep him safe till Monday," I said.

"And in the plane too," Angus replied.

The next day we rode again and Mr Miller told us that the flight was booked and Phantom would be flying with some brood mares on Monday evening. "It's a chartered flight," he said. "One of the mares can't go, so he'll be in a box by himself. I told them he was a heck of a horse. I sure hope he behaves."

I could think of nothing but the flight now. It seemed to dominate everything. I imagined a thousand things going wrong.

The Millers were wonderful. They took us swimming and to Charlottesville and to an outdoor concert. Pete and Phil came home on Sunday and we had a farewell dinner with wine, and an enormous rib roast, and fresh cornbread and gallons of ice cream, and salads of pineapple, mayonnaise, lettuce and cottage cheese. It was all very Virginian and I was suddenly overcome by the sadness of leaving. Virginia had never seemed so beautiful before, the Millers never nicer.

We were still up when the moon rose and the dark sky was filled with millions of stars like jewels on dark velvet.

"We'll be over in July," Pete told me. "It will sure be good to see you again."

I didn't want the day to end. I kept thinking,

I may never come again, this could be my last evening in Virginia.

Wendy wanted to know what she should wear in England. "Skirts are real short, aren't they?" she asked.

At last we retired to bed, but I couldn't sleep. It seemed impossible that this time tomorrow we would be flying to England with Phantom, it seemed too impossible to come true.

Pete and Phil had gone back to their military academy. The air was full of sounds unheard in England. I opened one of the windows and leaned out, remembering again the first time I had seen Phantom galloping wild and alone across the moonlit valley; somehow even then I had been certain that one day he would be mine.

8

Monday morning dawned fine.

"I'm coming with you. I'm not going to school," cried Wendy, leaping out of bed. "I want to see Phantom load. Dad does too."

I was dressing slowly, saying goodbye to everything, already feeling the heat of the sun through the windows. Angus was still asleep. Phantom had spent the night in the orchard and he was still there, scarred but sound, waiting by the gate. Mrs Miller helped us pack, putting everything in plastic bags with tissue paper between the folds. Tomorrow I shall be in England, I thought, and it still didn't seem possible.

"Charlie rang your parents," Mrs Miller told us. "And Charlie and Wendy are travelling with you to New York. The horse box is arriving after lunch."

There was a funny feeling in my stomach, as if it were full of fluttering butterflies.

"We can't possibly repay you for everything;

you've been tremendous," Angus said in a grown-up voice.

"We don't want repaying for anything, it's been a pleasure," replied Mrs Miller.

Annie was making cookies for us to eat on the journey. I felt then that the Millers were the best friends we had ever had, our only real friends.

I caught Phantom and groomed him. Then Angus and I went round the other horses saying goodbye. I stood for ages with my arms round Frances's neck, remembering the days and hours we had shared together. Then I said goodbye to Easter and Seashore and Pete's bay mare, and Pelican and Phil's new black hunter. Then I returned to Frances and said goodbye all over again. And all the while time was passing relentlessly and the worst part of the journey still lay ahead, waiting like some fearful ordeal to be overcome.

Lunch was hot dogs, followed by more ice cream. I wanted to ask Mr Miller for some money, but Angus said that we could beg no more and where was my pride? The day was at its hottest now; Phantom was sweating in the stable. Wendy found some slightly moth-eaten bandages in the saddle room and gave them to me. I put them on Phantom's forelegs. I was wearing jodhpurs and was far too hot. I was trying to look like a responsible person. Angus was dressed in grey trousers, a shirt and tie. Wendy wore jeans, moccasins and her favourite tee-shirt.

"It'll be kinda funny without you around," she said with a break in her voice.

"It will be funnier still to see you on our crabby little island," Angus replied, and we all laughed because he made England sound like our own private property.

Now the horse box was arriving across the cattle-grid to the yard. Annie was standing on the steps outside the laundry room waving goodbye.

"We should have got her some chocolates," muttered Angus.

"We'll send her something super from England, a jumper or something," I replied, and all the time I felt as though my heart was breaking, because I was leaving the dusty valley with the rock-hard ground and the Blue Ridge Mountains in the distance.

The driver of the horse box was letting down the ramp. He was a big, sweaty man in a grubby white shirt, which clung to his back in the heat, and light-coloured trousers.

"I'll take him," he said, looking at me.

I had led Phantom out by this time and he stood all flaxen and gold in the sunshine, bursting with health.

"He doesn't like strangers, let the kid lead

him up," said Mr Miller, who had appeared dressed in riding-clothes with a cloth cap on his head.

But Phantom would not budge. His head seemed to go higher and higher as though he was trying to look behind him and say goodbye to his beloved mountains. Angus fetched a scoop of oats. Annie appeared with carrots. Mrs Miller brought sugar. The driver took him, jerking at his head and shouting, "Get up there. Someone get a rope," he said presently. "Gee, he's strong."

They fetched a rope and put it round his buttocks and pulled, while I coaxed him with the scoop in front; but he threw himself backwards after a minute's contemplation and everyone fled.

"We'll never make it," said Mr Miller, looking at his watch. "What did I tell you, Jean? He's no darned good. Someone should put a bullet in him." I could feel the tears pricking behind my eyes. I couldn't imagine Angus and myself returning without him; it was awful beyond words.

Then I remembered something I had seen someone else doing at a show and I cried, "Let me ride him up. He trusts me."

Another minute and I was vaulting on his back while the driver was saying, "He'll kill her on the roof if he rears."

Angus was saying, "Be careful, Jean. Jump off if he goes up on his hind legs."

Phantom's coat was dark with sweat. I said, "Walk on," in the same voice as I used when I had lunged him months ago. I felt the tenseness going out of his body and I went on talking, but I can't remember what I said. I forgot the others completely; I could have been alone on a desert island – anywhere, I just continued talking and I sensed the others standing watching, no doubt thinking I was as nutty as a fruit-cake. And then slowly he moved. I went on talking and we were on the ramp and he was still walking forward, relaxed and confident, the fear drained out of him. I dismounted inside the box and someone put the ramp up. I tied up Phantom and shouted, "I'll stay here," and there were cries of "Goodbye and good luck."

It was a five-horse horse box and most of the partitions were still up, so there was not a lot of room. I heard the cab door close and the engine start. Angus looked at me through a window in the cab and said, "Are you all right?"

I was fighting back tears now; someone was still calling "Goodbye", and I should have been happy because the first part of the journey had begun and I was going home.

"Sure," I answered.

The drive was bumpy and I knew when we reached the highway because the box ran smoother. There were slats on the sides which I could peer through and I said goodbye to the drugstore where you could buy newspapers, writing paper, cosmetics, things you buy in a chemist's, and a host of other things, and have Cokes there too, and hot dogs, sitting at the tables in the centre of the store.

I said goodbye to the gas station where we bought our gas – petrol – and I heard the others talking on and on in a steady drone in the cab in front.

The drive to New York seemed to last for ever. Somewhere we all got out, except for Phantom, and stretched our legs in a side road, where small houses hid behind tall trees. Phantom kept whinnying as though he feared he would be forgotten. The driver mopped his brow.

"It'll be real hot in New York," he said.

We drove on and presently there was a feeling of evening outside and through the slats I could see people going home from work – dozens of men wearing sunglasses, women carrying shopping bags, girls in cotton dresses. Children were standing at the roadside and there was more and more traffic and larger and larger highways.

Angus passed some of Annie's cookies through the window between the cab and me. "Are you all right? Would you like to change places with me?" he asked.

I shook my head.

"It won't be too long now, Jean," Mr Miller told me.

"About another two hours," the driver said.

The rush-hour traffic was building up. There was driver after driver in white shirt, coat hanging up, listening to the car radio. Once I heard a train, another time a mother calling to her child. And now there were more houses and the fields were disappearing; then without warning, the suburban homes ceased and there were blocks and blocks of flats and skyscrapers and enormous gas stations. It's New York, I thought, we're nearly there.

Phantom was resting a hind leg. He looked peaceful enough. There was the smell of a town outside – petrol fumes, dust, hot pavements, rotting vegetables in dustbins, sweaty humans.

We kept stopping at traffic-lights and every time Phantom seemed to raise his head a little higher and grow more restless as though he too could smell the town outside. He looked very beautiful with his nostrils blown out and a wild look in his eyes.

Then, at last, the horse box started to slow down. I could see grass again through the trees and low buildings, and men in uniform, and hear the roar of aircraft taking off or landing.

"We've arrived," shouted Angus through the opening. "And there are some super planes."

I wasn't interested in the planes, only in one plane – Phantom's. I felt as though I had reached a turning point in my life, what Mum would call my "Waterloo".

We parked by some horse boxes. My legs were stiff when I stepped out into the summer dusk. Mr Miller took us across the airport to a buffet room and I remember I kept saying,

"What about Phantom? I don't want him scared."

"We've got an hour and a half before loading time. There's all sorts of formalities to be gone through yet. I'll see to them while you have something to eat," he replied.

Wendy brushed straw off my back. Angus was still raving over the planes, looking like grey monsters parked uneasily on the runways in the gathering dusk.

I ate two hamburgers without tasting them. Wendy and Angus talked. I don't know what they said. Then Wendy fell for a boy with dark hair and a lightweight summer suit. He had a smooth, sun-tanned face and looked like an advertisement for shaving cream. She whispered to me, "He's sure cute, isn't he?" in a perfectly audible voice, and the boy turned and smiled at us in a perfect ad for toothpaste and I felt slightly sick.

Quite soon after that he and Wendy were talking and Angus made a face at me and muttered, "Oh, to be in England." And then at last Mr Miller came back.

"The horse doctor is looking at him now," he said. "They're going to be loaded on pallets. There's a crowd of brood mares going too. It's so darned humid outside it isn't true."

The driver had unloaded Phantom. He stood like a wild horse, staring round the airport. His beauty made me catch my breath.

"Gee, some horse!" exclaimed Wendy.

"He's passed his tests," the driver said. "Sure you can hold him? He's real strong."

"Sure." I took the rope and we all walked together to where three brood mares were waiting patiently to be loaded, as peacefully as people waiting for a bus. Phantom neighed when he saw them and we were told to keep him away.

"Those mares are worth more than a million dollars," said a man unmistakably English.

The boxes were waiting on the ground and the mares walked into them without a murmur. A man asked Mr Miller for Phantom's certificates and Mr Miller passed him a handful of documents.

Then Phantom started to jump about and neigh, and the mares answered from their boxes. I felt panic growing inside me until I wanted to shout, Please hurry, every passing minute is going to make loading more difficult, but the official was still talking to Mr Miller.

Presently the driver went to the horse box and returned with Phantom's bridle. He had difficulty putting it on, because Phantom was whirling round and round by this time and his neck was streaked with sweat.

"I'll ride him in," I said before anyone could argue.

Angus legged me up and I could feel Phantom relaxing as I walked him round and round, staring at the light of New York beyond the airport.

A plane came in to land with a roar and he trembled all over and the reins were salt wet with his sweat. But he only stared at the plane and then relaxed as I rode him towards the box. There was a sudden silence as he walked into it; then behind me Angus shouted, "Hurray, well done, Jean!"

The Englishman said, "I've never seen that done before."

I dismounted and found I was trembling all over from nervous exhaustion. I took off Phantom's bridle, leaving his headcollar underneath.

I was allowed out of the box while the dolly took it to the aircraft standing ready on the runway; the dolly was rolled on to a lift and slowly Phantom was raised to the height of the aircraft and the box pushed inside on rollers fixed to the floor of the plane. It was then clipped into position inside. We all sighed with relief when that was done and Wendy said, "I owe you ten dollars – or was it twenty?"

And I said, "Fifty. Forget it." And none of us knew how to say goodbye.

Then Angus held out his hand and said, "It was good of you to come, sir. I don't know how to thank you."

And Mr Miller took it and squeezed it until Angus's face grew red with agony. "You're welcome, Angus. Proud to have known you," he said.

Then I held out my hand and received the same treatment, and suddenly Wendy's face was covered with tears and she walked away across the airport without saying goodbye.

I ran after her. I seized her arm and said, "I'm going to thank you for everything whether you like it or not. You've saved our lives countless times in countless ways, and it's impossible to thank you enough." It sounded silly, like a bad speech on Sports Day, and it didn't stop Wendy crying.

"You could have stayed a little longer," she muttered. "A few more days wouldn't have killed you."

I didn't know what to say. I thought I could hear the plane's engines starting up behind me and Angus was calling, "Come on, Jean."

"See you in July and thanks a million, million times for everything," I shouted.

Flying always thrilled me. I was filled with a wild excitement as I approached the plane. I thought of seeing England again, of leading Phantom into the yard at home, and I was filled with a sense of achievement. Mr Miller had handed Angus a mass of documents in a case. "You'll have to handle these," he said. "Jean can only think of that darned horse. Happy landings."

We watched him disappearing. "He's not walking out of our lives, none of them are," said Angus with a choke in his voice.

9

It was a long time before the plane took off. We had looked at the brood mares by then. They were thoroughbreds and one had a foal at foot. Phantom was screened off from them. Two seats had been provided for Angus and me. There was a haynet for Phantom and a polythene container full of water, and two containers of food for us.

When the plane took off at last I held him by his headcollar. We seemed to be going faster and faster and then miraculously we were airborne.

I kept saying, "Whoa, steady there," and I realised that other people were saying the same to the mares. It was a perfect take-off. Angus was wildly excited.

"New York looks wonderful," he cried. "I swear I can see Times Square and there's Manhattan and Wall Street . . . There are masses of lights. There's clouds," he said, "but not a lot, and stars, billions of stars."

We were really in the air now. Phantom started to munch his hay. I relaxed. I let my body go limp for the first time in hours. I was too tired to feel any great sense of triumph.

"It's so smooth," Angus said. "'We must be above the sea now." He kept disappearing and coming back with more information. I was fighting off sleep.

"There's a racehorse trainer on board," Angus told me. "All the grooms are English. The mares are travelling marvellously. It's practically dark and the clouds look like some fantastic ocean below us." He opened one of the food containers and handed me a sandwich. "You don't seem very excited," he said.

"It's smoother than anything I've ever been on before," I answered. "And I can't see much from here, can I?" All my strength seemed to have gone. I only wanted to sit by Phantom's head and wait for England.

"There's nothing to see at present," said Angus, disappearing and returning, "but one of the grooms says that sometimes you can see more than one sunrise."

"We've missed one of them," I said.

"You mean the New York one?" asked Angus.

I had finished my sandwich. Phantom was still eating.

"Wendy and Mr Miller will be just arriving

home in the horse box. Gee, they were swell, weren't they?" Angus said.

The temperature was regulated to suit the horses. I shivered more from fatigue than anything else.

"You go to sleep. I'll watch him. I'm not tired at all," Angus said, his eyes bright with excitement.

I shut my eyes and almost at once I was dreaming I was in Virginia again, chasing Wendy, who kept shouting, "You hate me. I know you do. You always have," and then suddenly it was England. The fields were full of hay bales which Wendy jumped and Mum was standing by a gate and clapping.

I don't know how long I slept. I dimly heard Angus talking about a sunset and Phantom pawing the floor, and English voices talking without pause as though telling their life histories. Then there was a noise like thunder and the plane seemed to tip and suddenly I was awake, sitting up, instantly aware of where I was. I leaped to my feet.

Phantom was racing round his box and Angus was trying to put his bridle on. But the plane wasn't flying straight any more and Phantom was standing on his hind legs and neighing. I heard someone shout, "For heaven's sake quieten that horse," before I snatched the bridle from Angus and threw the reins over Phantom's

head. Angus was holding on to his headcollar rope, but it didn't make much difference to Phantom, who seemed to have gone mad. I tried to hold his ear and failed, and for an awful minute or more I was whirling round the box with him, my legs entangled in the reins.

Then a voice said, "Let me help," and I saw the racehorse trainer for the first time, looking sombre in a coat and hat like someone from a different world. "We're eight miles up," he continued. "He'll finish us all off in a minute if he doesn't stop. One foot through the fuselage and we're done for."

I had forgotten what English voices sounded like. But his voice did nothing to calm Phantom, who threw himself against the side of the box and pawed the air, and suddenly I felt as terrified as he was – one hoof through the fuselage, I thought, and we are all finished. And I saw us going down into the sea, the wreck floating, while we had been sucked out into space. Mum and Dad hearing the news on television – the headlines in the papers. All this went through my mind in a flash but by then a man in uniform had appeared. "Put these on," he said, handing us oxygen masks. "It shouldn't be for long."

I couldn't get my mask on; my hands were shaking too much. But Angus knew how it went and pushed it over my head and clipped the ends together. The racehorse trainer had put his on and I saw that he was filling a hypodermic syringe. "I'll just give him a shot to quieten him down," he said.

Phantom was standing still now, looking rather drunk. His eyes looked glazed and his ears seemed to have no life in them. I put his bridle on. The plane was flying normally again.

"It was just a freak storm," the trainer said, slipping the syringe into Phantom's velvet skin. "Keep the bridle on for the rest of the flight, and stay with him. It's only another couple of hours." He was a big man, but he moved quietly and calmly round Phantom and one could tell he had spent most of his life with horses. He left us in the box and I heard him call, "Everything under control, Captain."

I looked at Angus and he smiled at me. My hands had stopped shaking but I felt sick. Presently a groom appeared and told us to take our masks off. He was a small, wiry man. "I've never known that happen before," he said. "Is he unbroken?"

"No, just difficult," Angus replied.

I did not feel like talking. Phantom looked half asleep. He moved unsteadily and his eyes were still peculiar. Angus had disappeared with the masks and presently he came back, saying, "I've just seen a sunrise. It's too late for England's. I don't know whose it is, but we're nearly home."

The night seemed to have lasted for ever. My teeth had started to chatter. Supposing Phantom goes mad again when we touch down I thought. But looking at him, I knew it wasn't possible, for he was too tired and dopey with the sweat drying on his sides and a faraway look in his eyes.

"We're nearly there," said the racehorse trainer. "I thought I would just let you know. You're a bit young to travel alone with a horse. I suppose they realised I was aboard so we would be all right. He's a nice little horse though, a real American I should say."

I started to tell him Phantom's life history, but there was not enough time.

"I must go now," he said. "We'll be landing soon. The best of luck with him."

"Thank you for saving us," I replied.

"You're welcome," he answered.

I left the hold for a moment and looked out and saw England below like patchwork, the fields and houses growing larger each moment. I started to feel sick again, with excitement this time, as though I had been away for years. Then I returned to Phantom and ate what was left of the food in the containers.

I knew we were losing height now but Phantom seemed hardly to notice. He stood like someone dreaming and he only moved a little as the plane started to reduce speed, going lower and lower until we were on the runway, still going but no longer in the air. Then almost without warning, we had stopped.

"They are going to unload your little horse last," the trainer said. "I'll keep an eye on him. You go and have a cup of coffee. He won't be out for half an hour at least."

I said, "Thank you."

Outside the grass looked very green and the sky grey, a greyer sky than we had seen for months. The Englishmen we saw looked lean and hard compared with Americans and the parked cars looked tiny. Everything seemed small, as though we had moved to somewhere which was made on a smaller scale.

"The air smells different," said Angus, sniffing. "And we haven't any money, have we? Not even to telephone. Oh cursed fate. And I would love bacon and eggs, wouldn't you?"

It was noon. It seemed impossible but somehow we had bypassed morning altogether. And then Angus cried, "Look, look over there. Beyond the barrier. There's Mum and Dad, look!" And suddenly we were both running as though our lives depended on it.

"It was a terrible journey," I shouted to Mum. "Phantom nearly took us to the bottom of the sea."

"You can't come out yet. What about Customs?" Dad asked.

We'd left our baggage in the plane and with it Angus's case of documents. We tore back to the runway. Some of the brood mares had been unloaded and were standing peacefully in the morning light like seasoned travellers waiting to be collected. Our luggage had been removed already, so we rushed back to Mum and Dad and I thought how marvellous it was to be with them again and how we needn't worry any more. Dad disappeared and came back with everything fixed up.

"You're coming with us," he said. "I've heard you were marvellous on the plane, as cool as cucumbers. But I think you've suffered enough for one night. Mr Price can load Phantom, there are plenty of people around to help and anyway he's still very docile after his tranquilliser. He shouldn't cause any more trouble."

Dad had bought a car. It looked very small and I couldn't imagine the Millers sitting in it. The motorway was full of traffic and it was much smaller than I remembered.

Later I found I had forgotten how high the hedges were, how small the cottages, how green the grass. I felt as though I was seeing England properly for the first time, but Angus fell asleep with his mouth open. Henley was full of traffic.

"It all looks so frightfully old," I said.

The trees were magnificent, large and thick with leaves and somehow terribly English. And all the time I still couldn't believe that we were really home, that somehow we had made it and that the night was over.

"The Millers are coming in July," I said. "They were super. Mr Miller and Wendy saw us off. They arranged everything. I don't know how we will ever repay them."

"There's no one nicer than a nice American," Dad said, "and Charlie always was a decent chap."

I knew every turn of the road; there was the

corner where I had fallen off Mermaid for the first time, the rectory where I had been to the annual Christmas party, the farm where we bought our hay and then the twisty stretch of road with high hedges and trees on each side which led home.

I couldn't sit still any longer. I wanted to walk the final bit, but Dad wouldn't stop the car. My heart started to pound against my ribs. Nothing had changed. The fields were as green as when we had left. There were birds singing in the trees, cow-parsley on the grass verges and low-branched apple trees in orchards. Then Dad turned into the familiar drive and I saw that Mermaid and Moonlight were home, grazing in the orchard.

"We thought Phantom might like to have a

little company so we begged them back," Mum said with a smile.

"We don't want any more night chases," Dad added.

The tulips were out and the rose climbing round the porch. It was all fantastically beautiful in a completely different way from the valley we had left. I wondered what the Millers would think of it when they came. Angus was awake now, climbing out of the car.

"What's the time?" he cried. "Can we ride before lunch?"

We ran together to the orchard and looked at Mermaid and Moonlight. "They're tiny," Angus said. "Much too small for us. I must have grown a mile since we were last here." He suddenly looked tired and disheartened. "I can't ride Moonlight any more. It would be cruelty to animals," he said.

Suddenly I felt sick again. I felt I had everything and it wasn't fair. "Can't we share Phantom? It was only luck that I found him. It might easily have been you," I answered.

Angus shook his head. He had his arms round Moonlight's neck. "He's yours. He always has been. I think he likes you. It's just one of those things. He and I would never get on. We are both too wild," he said.

"Perhaps Dad will buy you a new horse," I suggested.

"Not likely. It cost a fortune bringing Phantom over, and he's just bought a car. Oh, it doesn't matter," he finished, turning towards the house. But I knew it did matter by the way he walked, and suddenly everything was spoiled.

10

The next two months were busy. Phantom settled down. Angus and I attended the new comprehensive school, catching the bus each morning at the crossroads. I rode guiltily while Angus thought about his exams and tried not to mind. At weekends I schooled Phantom in the small paddock behind the house and Angus made a mock ring for me out of pieces of rope and string. We put peculiar things inside, old coats on sticks, an ancient pram with a heap of rags inside, a pile of stones.

One Saturday Angus dressed up and pretended to be a judge. He rang an ancient cowbell from Zermatt and shouted, "Will entries for Class Eight, Novice Jumping for Lunatics and the Infirm, please come into the ring."

Phantom hesitated for a moment and then walked in, only stopping to peer at the pram.

"Ride him round," shouted Angus, "and then give him a reward." Phantom cantered round the ring like a dressage horse, or so I told myself. Then I jumped off and gave him three lumps of sugar and a whole crust of bread. I tied him up and made a few jumps – poles perched on dented oil drums, a wall out of the old scullery door, frightful crossbars out of bean poles which were far too fragile for a decent jump. Angus found a mackintosh and put it on the poles, then he brought out two chairs and tied some string between them and attached Mum's tea-towels to it with clothes-pegs.

"I'm not very happy about jumping the chairs. I know they are only the kitchen ones, but all the same . . ." I said.

"You need only jump it once," Angus replied. "He never hits anything anyway."

He started telling me how to jump the course while I untied Phantom and mounted. The sky was full of fluffy clouds and there was a breeze which fanned my face.

Phantom cleared the pole in the air easily. He hesitated for a moment at the scullery door and then we were over that too. He looked at the mackintosh and jumped very big and then we cantered on towards the chairs. I could feel him eyeing the tea towels. They were rather gaudy, one had an elephant on it, another flowers, the third a pepper-pot and carving knife and fork. He tried to run out, but I managed to straighten him and even now I don't know exactly what went wrong. Angus said afterwards that he turned as he jumped. I was nervous and I've always felt he knew it. Anyway, one of his hoofs caught in a chair and there was the sound of cracking wood and Angus started to shout, "Stop him, you fool. Get off."

I threw myself on to the ground but it was too late, for the chair was already a heap of broken wood on the grass.

"I told you we shouldn't use them," I cried. "I knew something awful would happen."

"You didn't ride him properly," shouted Angus, picking up the tea towels which were covered with hoof marks.

"We should have touched wood," I replied. "Whatever will Mum say?"

I turned Phantom into the orchard and rushed indoors with the tea towels. I started to wash them at the sink and Mum appeared.

"Whatever are you doing that for?" she asked. "They were clean ten minutes ago. And where are two of the kitchen chairs? I've been looking everywhere for them. I've just had a call from the Millers; they are coming at the end of the month. We'll need the chairs then, because there aren't enough for us all in the dining-room."

"We've broken one of them. We were using them for jumps," Angus explained. "I'll buy you a new one. I've got some money in my building society account."

"They were forty pounds each," Mum cried, running towards the paddock.

She came back slowly with the pieces of wood in one hand, the good chair in the other. I felt horribly guilty. Angus kept saying, "I'll buy you another. I'll go into Oxford or Reading on the bus. I'll get you something super from an antique shop."

"It's not as though you're only nine or ten," Mum said. "You should know better. Why don't you take Phantom to the riding-school? I'm sure Miss Mackintosh will let you jump her jumps."

I had learned to ride at the riding-school. Miss Mackintosh was small and weatherbeaten. She had worn her hair the same way for twenty years and she was quite old now and it didn't suit her any more. But she was kind, one of the kindest people I had ever met.

"What a super idea. I'll go after lunch," I said.

"And there's a show coming up. You can take the Millers," Mum continued. "I've rung up for a schedule."

"Oh, you're wonderful," I cried. "The most wonderful mother in the world! I shall take Phantom. I shall make him go in the ring and win Mr Miller's bet." I was dancing about with excitement now. I rushed outside with the tea towels and hung them on the line. Phantom was standing under the trees with Moonlight and

Mermaid. I caught him and groomed him for forty minutes, and oiled his hoofs. It was lunchtime after that and Angus and I washed up afterwards because Mum was tired and we still felt guilty about the chairs. Then I tacked up Phantom and rode down the road towards the riding-school, wondering whether the pound had gone up or down recently and how many dollars made a pound.

Miss Mackintosh was tacking up horses for the afternoon ride. She squinted up at me before she cried, "But it's Jean. You are back, and what are you riding? He's lovely."

She stood back as horsy people do when they want to look at a horse properly, and she said, "He carries himself beautifully, and he's got a wonderful shoulder. Where did you find him?"

"I brought him back with me," I said, and started to tell his story.

"I can't hear it all now," she said after a minute. "I've got a class in ten minutes; but knowing you, you want to jump."

"Please. Are you sure? I mean, it seems an awful cheek," I began.

"This way," said Miss Mackintosh, walking towards the five-barred gate which led to the jumping field.

"I'll put them at three foot to start with. Has he jumped that high? Or would you rather start with the cavaletti?"

"Three foot will be fine." I rode Phantom in a circle. He had never jumped proper painted showjumps before, for the ones in Virginia were plain, permanent, solid fences to test hunters across country.

"Ready?" called Miss Mackintosh. I tightened Phantom's girth and called back, "Yes."

The jumps were arranged in a figure of eight. The first one was a Sussex gate. Phantom took it in his stride; the wall came next and he cleared that too. I turned right for the red and white crossbars and he increased his speed and suddenly we were tearing round the course, one jump following another, his tail streaming behind him like a pennant and Miss Mackintosh jumping about in the middle, shouting, "Not so fast. They're nothing to him. I'll put them up a foot."

"But that will make them four foot," I said, drawing rein.

"So what?" she said. "If you want to jump him in classes he'll have to clear four foot. You had better register him, you've got a winner there." Her face was lit up with excitement. And I was filled with gratitude.

"There's a show in three weeks' time. You can come with me. I'm only taking two in the box," she said.

I trusted Miss Mackintosh completely. Anything and everything seemed possible as I rode round the course again. Phantom didn't let me down. I sat on top and he took me round, jumping every fence perfectly, turning the corners like a polo pony.

"He's worth three thousand without a doubt," said Miss Mackintosh, when I had dismounted and she was stuffing Phantom with oats from her pockets. "You are a very lucky girl. Ring up the show secretary tonight and see if they are taking any more entries, then ring me and let me know. There's a schedule pinned to the wall in the saddle room."

The yard was full of waiting pupils when I reached it. I put Phantom in a box and helped adjust their stirrups. Miss Mackintosh's words still rang in my ears. "He's worth three thousand without a doubt."

I went round the stables with a skip and filled up the water buckets, remembering how I had haunted the stables once, and feeling immensely grateful for what Miss Mackintosh had taught me in the past.

Then, after finding a piece of paper in the saddle room and writing down the show secretary's telephone number, I rode home along the grass verges. Cars slowed down for Phantom and an enormous lorry stopped completely and then eased itself past us at five miles an hour, while Phantom stood like a statue eyeing it. I'm winning that battle too, he's getting used to traffic, I thought, cantering along the verge, jumping ditches and singing, imagining the Millers arriving and loving everything.

The next day was spent turning out the cottage in preparation for the arrival of the Millers. Dad bought a gallon of white emulsion paint and three big brushes. We spread paper on everything and Angus and I helped paint walls and ceilings. When we had finished we had paint in our hair and on our faces. Mum was painting the doors in the kitchen with a blue gloss paint. "There won't be much for lunch," she said. "Open a tin of corned beef and there's some lettuces in the garden. We'll have a proper dinner tonight."

"I can't think why we have to bother so much about the Millers," Angus said. "Wendy always calls England a crabby little island, so they won't be expecting much, will they?"

I wandered into the garden and found the lettuces our tenants had obligingly planted some time back in the spring. Next week we would start exams, and we weren't prepared for them. If I fail them all I shall take up riding, I thought. I'll school horses and sell them. I'll tour the shows and sleep in the other half of a trailer on a camp-bed. I shall never pass the history exam, nor the geography for that matter.

On my way back I brushed against the door Mum had been painting and my shirt had blue all down one side. Then Angus tripped over the emulsion paint and we spent nearly an hour mopping it up with newspaper and rags, and we all had nerves about the Millers' impending visit.

"We'll never be able to amuse them," Angus said. "We haven't any mountains round the corner, nor half a dozen horses to spare, and you can't ask Phil and Pete to play games."

"I don't see why not," answered Mum. "Anyway, there's the show. They'll enjoy that."

"Will they?" replied Angus. "I don't think

they will. They'll think English horses are tiny."

"And I shall fall off or run away and then I shall have to pay Mr Miller five hundred dollars and I haven't got that much money in the world," I cried and suddenly everything seemed against me again, the exams, Phantom, the painting and clearing up. "I don't believe we'll ever be ready for them. Where are they going to sleep?" I asked.

"Charlie and Ann can have our room," Mum said. "Dad and I will have the spare room, Wendy can share your room, Jean, and the boys can have Angus's room and Angus, you can sleep in the summerhouse."

"But it leaks," yelled Angus. "Haven't you noticed, the deckchairs are all wet?"

"I'll have to patch it up then," replied Mum.

"And what about food, Mum?" I asked. "You've no idea how much they eat. They'll eat us out of house and home!"

I wanted to see them again; but the preparations were spoiling everything. Mum insisted that all the chair covers had to be washed as well as the bed covers. Angus and I shampooed the carpets; then we polished the brass, and I hardly schooled Phantom at all.

I failed the geometry exam completely. I got twenty out of a hundred for maths, and forty for French. The weather changed and there were days of endless rain and I imagined the Millers, wrapped up in mackintoshes, saying, "Your crabby English weather!" Finally we both had a chemistry exam. I could only answer three questions out of twenty-two, but Angus managed eight.

Dad raged about our exam results and threatened us with a cramming school, and Angus said that since he had only passed in English and Geography, he had better be a dustman. Then Dad hired someone to coach us in the holidays and I imagined the Millers peering over our shoulders while a bearded teacher talked to us in French.

Angus was very bad-tempered. He said there was no point in living if we were going to be coached all through the summer holidays, and that he was going to commit suicide while the Millers were staying so that everyone in the world would know what awful lives English children lived. "It's nothing but education from the cradle till middle age," he shouted.

The orchard was soaking wet and so was the paddock and there was hardly any time to ride. Dad saw the headmaster and we were given extra homework for the holidays; and still it rained. I wondered what I could sell to pay Mr Miller when Phantom refused to enter the ring. I had two cups which I had won on Moonlight, but neither was silver so they were not worth much. I had some books and an opal necklace my godmother had left me, but I decided not to sell that, even though I didn't wear it.

We knew that the Millers would soon be on their way, and Angus started to complain about the sheets. "They have super ones, different colours for each room," he said.

"And gallons of ice cream," I said. "They can't live without ice cream, Mum, and saying, 'Hi, what about a Coke?' And they don't like orange squash, only orange juice," I added.

Mum was as nervous as we were. She ordered a turkey and a whole leg of ham and she found tins of cold iced tea in the supermarket, with everything in it but the ice.

The last few days passed far too fast. We started to count blankets and sheets. Then Mermaid developed laminitis and would not move at all, and for an awful three hours until the vet came we thought she had something else and would have to be put down. After that Angus spent every spare moment walking her up and down and she had to be kept in the stable and mucked out every morning before school.

Then Dad suggested that we could take the Millers to play tennis on the village courts so we rushed into Henley and bought three more racquets, because mine had decayed while we were in Virginia. And then all too soon it was the day before the Millers' arrival, and we moved Angus's bed into the summerhouse and tried in vain to patch the roof.

Dad had had the car washed and serviced by this time and had bought vast quantities of whisky, vermouth and Coca-Cola. The house looked spotless, more like a hotel, I thought, than a house where people actually lived. Term had ended but the thought of our tutor hovering over us during lovely summer mornings saying, "How can E equal C, when D doesn't equal B?" hung over us like a huge black shadow.

11

The telephone was ringing. Dad was mowing the lawn. Mum had gone to the village shop to buy some butter.

"You get it," said Angus. "I've got to dig some potatoes for lunch."

I ran into the hall and picked up the receiver, and a voice said, "Hi there. It's Wendy. We've arrived. We're in Reading."

"In Reading?" I exclaimed. "Already?"

"Sure. The plane landed early."

"We'll come and fetch you. We'll be there in about forty minutes, allowing for traffic hold-ups," I said, wondering if there would be enough lunch for them all.

"Don't be nuts," cried Wendy. "Dad's getting a hire car for us right now. I say, isn't your little island cute? I love your hedges but there's more barbed wire than we've got back home."

"Sure," I answered.

"Here's Pete," Wendy said. There was a sound of giggling and Pete took over. "Hiya,

Jean," he said. "We sure like it over here; it's some place. Here's the old man with the car, be seeing you."

I put down the receiver and rushed outside. "They've arrived," I yelled. "They're on their way. Where's Mum?"

Dad had stopped mowing the lawn. "Where are they?" he asked calmly.

"Reading!" I cried. "They're on their way in a hire car."

"How super!" cried Angus. "I shall be able to stop thinking about education for a whole week. I'll dig some more potatoes. Who did you talk to?"

"Wendy and Pete. They seem to like our crabby little island," I replied. "I think I'd better switch the electric blankets on in their beds; they're sure to find English beds damp."

"Keep calm," Dad said. "Don't panic. I'll get out the drinks and some ice. Is there enough lunch?"

"I don't know till Mum's back," I shouted.

"Why are you shouting?" asked Dad. "It's not very ladylike."

The rain had stopped. A wind blew the trees. It was a typical summer day in England.

I started to scrape the potatoes; then Mum returned.

"I hear they are on their way, and there's only casseroled beef and ice cream," she said.

"I've dug some more potatoes," Angus said coming in, his hands covered with earth. "I don't know why you're fussing. Can't we just have hot dogs and cider? I don't think they've tasted cider before. Has anyone got a fiver? I'll go and get some."

We were still one chair short in the kitchen, but I didn't mention it. Angus disappeared in search of cider, I finished scraping potatoes. Mum added some chopped-up bacon to the stew. Dad was washing his hands upstairs. He had a week's leave from work and had spent the last few days doing what he called "Putting the garden straight."

Mermaid was still in the stable with laminitis. We had hung our few rosettes in the saddle room and cleaned all the tack. I was wearing jeans and a blouse. Mum wanted me to change. "They won't be in jeans," she said.

"They usually are, and they are not relative," I answered, "and they're used to me in jeans. Honestly, Mum, must I dress up for the Millers?"

"Oh all right. But I'm going to change," she said, going upstairs. "Watch the potatoes."

"They are coming through the village now," yelled Angus, with a bottle of cider in each hand. "I saw them."

"You welcome them. I'm still changing," shouted Mum.

I rushed down the garden path as they were climbing out of the car. "Hiya," I yelled. "Nice to see you."

"Heavenly day! Isn't it cute?" cried Mrs Miller. "But are you sure you can fit us all in, Jean?"

"Where's Phil?" I asked.

"He went on up to London. He's got a girl-friend there. He's staying with her family. You know Phil," replied Wendy, laughing.

"How's the wild horse? You made it then?" asked Mr Miller.

Dad had appeared now. "Come and have something to drink, Charlie," he said. "You must need it. I expect the kids want to see the ponies."

"We're not kids any more." I said. Do you want to see Mermaid and Moonlight and Phantom?" I asked Wendy and Pete. "There's a show the day after tomorrow, I'm taking Phantom."

"It's all so green," Pete said.

"You didn't crash in the ocean then?" Wendy asked. "It's been kinda quiet back home without you."

Before lunch Dad whispered "FHB", which meant "family hold back", so Angus and I were not to ask for second helpings. Mr and Mrs Miller admired everything. They said that the cottage was full of antiques and that they would sure like to take the whole lot back to Virginia with them. Wendy said that the cottage would be great as a guest-house.

They looked too large for the dining-room, which had been built five hundred years ago when humans were several inches smaller than us, much less than the Millers.

In the afternoon we played clock-golf on the lawn and talked. Mum cooked an enormous dinner and Dad opened two bottles of wine and we all got rather silly. Mr Miller kept talking about Phantom. "If you get that horse into a ring the day after tomorrow, I'll give you five hundred dollars, but if you don't, I sure expect the same from you. That's how I remember it. Am I right?" he asked.

"Yes," I said.

Mum suddenly looked rather pale. And Dad said, "Let's have coffee next door, shall we?" and stood up. He shot a piercing glance at me, and I realised that this was the first time he had heard of the bet. I mouthed "Opals" at him but he simply shrugged his shoulders and shepherded the Millers into the sitting-room.

I put the kettle on for the coffee and Pete said, "Don't worry, Jean, I'll pay it. I'm loaded with dollars."

And I heard myself reply in rather a haughty voice, "I always pay my debts and I wouldn't dream of borrowing from you. I've got some jewellery," and all the time I was feeling colder and colder and wishing that I had spent more time schooling Phantom rather than shampooing carpets and painting ceilings.

Wendy and I talked for hours that night. The next day the Millers planned to go to Stratford. They wanted us to go too, but in the end only Angus could go, because I had to spend the day getting Phantom ready for the show. Miss Mackintosh rang up and we were to leave the riding-school at half past eight in the morning. Wendy and Pete had promised to help but neither of them could plait a mane, since they had a man at home called Joe who always prepared their horses for shows.

Presently the Millers left in their car. It was a large estate and Dad suddenly decided to go as well as Angus, to show them the way.

I helped Mum with the washing-up and she said that she thought they were enjoying themselves all right and that after Saturday they were going back to London and then to visit long-lost relations in Ireland. "But why did you agree to that silly bet with Mr Miller?" she asked, drying a plate. "You know we can't afford five hundred dollars. You must be mad; it's more than three hundred pounds. I can't think what he's thinking of either."

"I'll just have to sell my opals," I answered.

"What, today? Anyway, you shouldn't think of it. Your godmother left them for you to wear when you're grown up."

"There's nothing else I can do; besides of course, to win," I added quickly.

"Then you'd better win," said Mum, making a face at me.

I caught Phantom and schooled him. I concentrated on making him more obedient to my legs. I did turns on the forehand, half passes, and turns on the haunches. Then I did a full pass at the trot and, with rising spirits, I thought that perhaps he had got the makings of a dressage horse. I shall be able to ride him in horse trials. I rode him out of the orchard gate and down the road and turned right towards the riding-school, and here the grass and nettles on the verges nearly met across the narrow road. It was a damp English summer morning with the hay cut and carried and the crops of oats, wheat and barley still green in the fields. Small boys were riding an assortment of bikes up and down the road. They shouted, "Ride him, cowboy," and I remembered how Angus had been like that once, small and grubby and mad on his bike, saying a hundred times a day, "Can I go out on my bike? Please, Mum?" And I, even then, tangle-haired, small, constantly in dew-drenched trainers, could think of nothing but riding.

The riding-school was full of pupils when I reached it. "There's no one in the jumping paddock. Try your luck," said Miss Mackintosh. "But don't jump more than a dozen jumps or you'll make him stale."

I rode Phantom round a three foot course and he jumped it easily, only touching one pole which didn't fall. I had entered for the sixteen and under class, which was open.

"See you tomorrow at eight-thirty. Don't be late," called Miss Mackintosh as I left, pushing her way through a crowd of pupils.

I felt old now. It seemed years since I had been a small child treating Miss Mackintosh as a sort of god. I let Phantom walk home on a loose rein and he ignored the cars which passed. Well, that's one battle completely won, I thought. I put him in Mermaid's loose box, which is built of brick and flint, but more flint than brick, and thought we'd have to find homes for Moonlight and Mermaid. It wasn't fair to keep them when we never rode them.

I found Mum washing lettuce in the sink.

"We're only having a light lunch," she said, and then, "How did he go?"

"Like a dream," I said. "He's too marvellous to be real. But I feel awful about it, because Angus can't ride at all. I think we'll have to sell Moonlight and Mermaid and buy something for him."

"They would be lovely to breed from," Mum answered. "Miss Croft has got an Arab stallion and the fee is quite small, and Mr Pratt says we can rent his field."

I imagined two foals cantering about the orchard on long legs. "It's just an idea," Mum said.

"A fabulous one," I cried. "Absolutely fantastic." But it still didn't solve Angus's problem of having no horse to ride.

I spent the afternoon washing Phantom's tail, grooming him until, had he been a piece of furniture, I would have been able to see my face in him. Then I put my grooming things ready in Mum's shopping basket for the next morning and started on my tack, but all the time I could feel panic growing inside me. I saw Phantom standing on his hind legs, spinning round as he had in Virginia, galloping away, myself just a passenger again. I had decided to put his drop noseband a hole tighter, but it would not stop him rearing. I saw myself abjectly saying to Mr Miller, "I'm so sorry I can't pay you yet. But I can when I've sold my opals."

And Mr Miller would say, "Forget it. It sure doesn't matter." And he would go home to Virginia saying that English people didn't pay their debts.

I'll say I've got the money in my building society account, I decided, and then I started to wonder for the first time how much my opals were worth.

But now the Millers were coming back, laughing as they came up the garden path. "Gee, it was great," Wendy cried. "I sure wanted to be hunting across Warwickshire; those hedges are something. How do they grow so straight?"

I put my girth on top of my saddle. It still needed whitening, but that would have to wait till later. Pete came straight round to the saddle room. "I sure wished you had come," he said. "Do you need any help? I've got a pair of strong arms."

"No, thanks all the same," I said. "Did you have a good time?"

"Sure, it was great," he said, putting an arm round my shoulders. "But I guess you had a miserable time worrying about that silly bet with the old man, huh?"

I nodded slowly.

"And I reckon your opals aren't worth five hundred dollars."

I shook my head.

"Why don't you call the whole thing off?" he suggested. "The old man expects you to. But he won't make the first move."

I could see myself saying, "I agree with what you said, I don't think Phantom will ever go into a ring, here or in Virginia, so please can we call off our bet?" I imagined him holding out his hand saying, "Now you're talking sense, Jean." And the whole scene was so completely foreign to my nature that I felt like shouting, "No, no, no, I would rather die." But I didn't. I shrugged my shoulders and said, "I'm going to win it. You're all in for a surprise."

Then I hastily touched wood and Pete saw me and said, "You've thought that before. You were real certain you were going to show everyone back home. Be smart, quit now while you've got the chance. No one will despise you for it."

Suddenly I was hating him for not believing me. "I don't want to talk about it any more," I cried, walking towards the cottage. "If I can't pay, Dad will have to. We'll sell the family silver, we have our pride."

"A real silly word, pride," shouted Pete. "And where's the silver? I haven't seen any."

My eyes were suddenly brimming with tears because again he didn't believe me. "Turn the spoons over and look," I yelled. "They're silver and they're old and there are twelve of them – and then there are the knives and forks and soup spoons." We're quarrelling, I thought, and it's never happened before.

Everything had suddenly turned sour. I could hardly speak a word throughout dinner, and the food nearly choked me. I kept looking at Pete and thinking, you traitor! How could you have said such things?

Once I caught him looking at the handle of a teaspoon and he blushed.

149

Angus seemed weary and soon retired to the summerhouse. It was raining and I was unable to amuse Wendy, for now I could think of nothing but tomorrow.

Finally the Millers decided to watch television with Mum and Dad and I wandered to bed feeling a failure in more ways than one. I pretended to be asleep when Wendy appeared muttering, "Crabby English weather."

The words Pete had said: "Where's the silver? I haven't seen any," echoed over and over in my brain. They were stupid enough words, but I felt they were weighted with everything he thought about us, and it was like a sledgehammer hitting some tender spot in my brain again and again.

12

The weather was fine when I climbed out of
bed next morning, dressing quietly so as not to
wake Wendy, stopping to pray for one brief moment that Phantom would enter the ring and
not let me down. When I went outside the sun
was rising above the trees. Phantom was lying
down, looking like a prince, with Mermaid
watching over him.

He let me put on a headcollar before he
stood up and shook himself. Cocks were crow-
ing everywhere and there was a continuous
chorus of birdsong from the trees. The grass
was still wet and my jeans were soaked up to
the knee by the time I had reached the stable.
Outside the road was empty. The whole countryside at this moment seemed to belong to me
and the birds and, of course, Phantom.

At seven o'clock I was eating breakfast in the
kitchen. Phantom was ready by this time. When
I was struggling into my boots a sleepy Angus
appeared from the summerhouse, still in his

pyjamas with a cobweb in his tousled hair.

"Do you want any help? Have you got everything? Don't let us down. You know your opals probably aren't worth five hundred dollars?" he said.

"I know, I've been told," I answered.

Riding along the road towards the riding-school I felt panic coming back. I must think of something else, of school, of Mermaid in foal; but I couldn't. I could only imagine Mr Miller waiting for his money. The post van was coming down the road and I could see cows being turned into a meadow after milking. Phantom was carrying himself marvellously. I felt as though we were trotting on air.

The trailer was waiting in the yard, its ramp down, when I reached the riding-school. Miss Mackintosh appeared in breeches and boots, white shirt, tie and hairnet. "It's going to be a glorious day," she said. "I'll load mine first."

She led out a big chestnut with two white socks behind. I wondered how she mounted so big a horse as she led him towards the trailer. Three minutes later I was leading Phantom up the ramp, talking to him, saying, "This is our great day. You must behave."

Miss Mackintosh put the ramp up. "So far, so good," she said. "I'll just get my hat and coat and then we're off."

"Mum and Dad are bringing oats and

grooming things," I said, putting my saddle and bridle in Miss Mackintosh's Range Rover.

I sat in the front. The journey took an hour or more and was uneventful, except that my legs had started to feel like jelly.

The show was in a stadium – there were no green trees, no open space; Only the trains tearing along a track fifty metres away, and tarmac, and dusty earth and cars. "No one told me it was here," I cried. "Phantom will never go in. He will think it's a trap. Why didn't someone tell me it was in a stadium?"

"It was on the schedule," Miss Mackintosh replied.

"It must have been in jolly small letters then," I said.

"Keep calm and he'll keep calm," suggested Miss Mackintosh. She was riding her chestnut in the Novice Jumping for Grade C Horses. I left Phantom in the trailer and watched the hacks being judged. The sun was shining and at the moment there were only a few people in the tiers of seats round the stadium.

After a time I unboxed Phantom and tied him to the outside of the trailer and polished him with the stable rubber. I was feeling sick now. I simply couldn't imagine Phantom going into the stadium. I tacked up and walked him up and down, letting him look at everything. My class was at ten-thirty and the fourteen and under jumping was in progress. Phantom was too big for it.

I had never ridden in so large a show before. I cursed myself for entering without reading the front of the schedule and found myself longing for the small, cosy gymkhanas at which I had competed so often on Moonlight; where the first prize was ten pounds and everyone knew everyone else.

But now my parents and Angus and the Millers had arrived. "Some show," shouted Wendy. "Phantom looks great, and so do you," called Pete, no doubt trying to make up for the unpleasantness of the evening before. They looked very American, and I think quite a few people immediately decided I was American too.

"If you think Phantom's going in that stadium you're even nuttier than I ever imagined," Mr Miller told me.

I shrugged my shoulders. Secretly I agreed with him – it seemed impossible that Phantom would ever canter round the green turf with people watching on all sides – but I wasn't going to let Mr Miller know. I was determined to keep up the pretence of being able to do it till the last minute of defeat.

Dad patted Phantom and said quietly, "Don't let us down, Jean. Ride as though our lives depended on it."

The winner of the fourteen and under jumping was coming out of the ring with a cup in her hand. If only it was over, I thought, if only I could go home and bury my head in some sand and never see the Millers again.

Pete pulled up my girth. "You were sure right about the spoons," he said. "You've got plenty and they're all silver."

But now the spoons didn't matter any more. The whole of the evening before was trivial compared with what was going on in the ring, for now men were putting up the jumps. There were eleven of them and they were going up to three foot six at least.

"You look a bit green," said Angus, glancing at me with a nervous smile lurking behind his eyes. "Shall I lead him up to the entrance when the moment comes?"

"If you like." I felt indifferent, somehow removed from it all now. I think that I simply couldn't face the suspense any more and had temporarily switched some part of myself off.

"They are calling you into the collecting ring," Mum told me. "All the luck in the world, darling."

She was wearing a cotton suit and sling-back sandals.

"The same from here," cried Mrs Miller. "And don't you go worrying about Charlie's bet. Heavenly day, we don't expect you to pay five hundred dollars."

"I won't pay because I'm going in. But anyway, I always pay my debts."

Brave words! They seemed to come from a long way off. It wasn't really me speaking, but someone else, some ancestor braver than myself speaking for me.

I told the collecting-ring steward my number. It was thirteen.

"Thirteen!" shouted Wendy. "Gee whizz!"

Angus held Phantom while I walked the course. Surveying the jumps I felt sicker every second. There was a terrible combination of three, an enormous wall, a spread of parallel bars which seemed wider than any jump I had ever imagined and, finally, a water jump. If it wasn't for the five hundred dollars I would be happy to remain outside, I thought, mounting again.

"Some jumps," Wendy said. "They sure look big – like Madison Square Garden."

I started to talk to Phantom. "We are going in there," I said. "It isn't a corral, there's nothing to worry about. Look, ponies are going in and coming out without any trouble; there's nothing to it." People were looking at me now but I ignored them. Phantom cocked an ear back and listened. I can't remember all I said, I just continued in the same voice, talking and stroking his neck.

Angus pulled off his tail bandage. "You're next," he said. "Good luck."

The collecting steward said, "Ready? All right, go in, but wait for the bell."

I could see the crowd in tiers of seats round the ring. Mr Miller was out there somewhere watching, so were Mum and Dad. Phantom was walking forward now, calmly, his neck arched. He played with his bit and dropped his nose and suddenly we were in the ring, trotting

round waiting for the bell, and all my fear had
gone, to be replaced by a feeling of immense
confidence.

I prayed for the bell to ring soon and it did.
I closed my legs against Phantom's sides and we
were cantering towards the first jump. Phantom

slowed down and for one terrible moment I thought he was going to refuse, something he had never done before. Then it was behind us and we were cantering towards the next fence, a road-closed sign, and now he was taking over. He didn't hesitate. In midair he seemed to kick his hind legs even higher and then we were racing on towards the parallel bars. After that came the wall, the gate, the fearsome combination where he took off too early for the last fence and scraped the top and there was an "Oh" from the crowd, but it didn't fall. There were crossbars and a stile and another jump I hardly noticed, then there was only one more jump now before the water. I slowed him down a little and then we were over that too, racing towards the water. Don't let go yet, Jean, I thought, you're nearly clear, steady, steady, and then we were over and from the stands came a tremendous burst of clapping and I fell forward on Phantom's neck, patting him and saying over and over again, "We've done it."

"You're the only clear round so far," cried Angus, rushing to meet me.

"It was great," cried Pete. "You've won the bet."

"Gee, Pete, as if she doesn't know," cried Wendy.

A voice quite near said, "They're Americans. They must have come over especially. I bet she ends up jumping for the United States."

"Actually I'm English," I said, turning round. "These are my friends from America. If I jump for any country it will be England."

They looked embarrassed.

"There's a jump-off," Dad said. "Well done, Jean."

Mr Miller held out an envelope. "It's yours, Jean," he told me. "You've sure earned it."

I didn't know what to say. At last I managed, "It's too much. You've done so much for us already."

"Exactly," agreed Dad, trying to push away his hand.

"I pay my debts," replied Mr Miller. "This girl was prepared to sell her necklace to pay hers. I sure don't have to."

"Please don't, Charlie," pleaded Mum.

"Take it, Jean," said Mr Miller, pushing it into my hand. "And don't ever let it be said that Virginians don't pay their gambling losses."

"They are putting up the jumps," Angus said. "You'll be going first in the jump-off."

I rode in with the five hundred dollars in my pocket for luck. Phantom danced a little and looked at the crowds, as though this time he knew they were there watching him. Then the bell sounded and we were cantering towards the first fence and as he jumped I suddenly knew what I would spend the money on – a horse for

Angus, who was standing in the wings watching, a stable rubber in his hand. Phantom knocked the next fence, probably because my mind wasn't with him, for at that moment I was seeing a new horse coming to live at Sparrow Cottage.

The course was six inches higher except for the water jump which remained the same, but I didn't notice it. We went faster this time and Phantom raced over the combination with a tremendous flourish as if to make up for rapping a fence last time. And now once again we were racing for the water, and I sensed the tenseness of the crowd, the sudden hushed silence, which was quiet enough to let me hear the drone of an aeroplane overhead. Phantom took off too early, but it didn't matter for he had no intention of getting his hoofs wet. There was a burst of applause and I knew we were clear. I put my reins in one hand and, cantering out, I could hear a train and Angus yelling, "Well done."

This time Miss Mackintosh was there to greet me too. "What an achievement!" she cried. "Well done, Jean."

I leaped off to find oats in my pockets for Phantom. The other clear round was going in now – a boy on a chestnut as lean as himself. "Don't hurry him, let him look," said his mother, small and plump in dark glasses.

"It was a pity you hit the second fence," said Miss Mackintosh. "What happened?"

I remembered that she had always been keen on post-mortems. "I was thinking of something else," I said.

She made a tut-tutting noise.

The sun was shining on us all now and I longed to take off my coat. We could not see the whole ring, but someone said, "He's over the first three clear."

Angus started twisting the stable rubber into knots and biting his nails. A voice said, "Is your horse for sale? Because if he is, I would like to make an offer."

I shook my head and turned to see a man

running his sharp eyes over Phantom. "I'll give you four thousand."

"I'm afraid he's not for sale. I'm keeping him for ever," I said.

"He's hit the combination, he's stopped, the boy's fallen off," shouted Angus. "You've won."

The Millers were running down the steps from the stands. The boy was coming out leading his chestnut. Angus was jumping up and down.

"Number twenty-five has been eliminated," announced the loudspeaker.

Angus pulled up my girth. Dad started stroking Phantom's neck. Mum said, "You've won."

Pete said, "Holy smoke! I never knew he

could jump like that. You wait till I tell them back home."

"They won't believe you," I replied, suddenly seeing the valley again in my imagination – the parched earth, the mountains in the distance, the Millers' house, the people saying, "Sure, but we don't believe you. That little horse will never make good, no sirree."

"Oh yes they will," answered Pete. "I've got it all here real good. I brought a roll of film. I'll be sending it to the newspapers. I'll let the whole of Virginia know."

I wanted to say, "You're fantastic," but at that moment the loudspeaker announced, "Will the following numbers come into the ring: Number thirteen, Miss Jean Simpson on Phantom . . ."

I was riding in now and somewhere a band was playing. Phantom danced and tossed his head and I kept remembering the first time I had seen him galloping wild and alone across the moonlit valley. It all seemed to have happened years ago. I halted in the centre of the ring and the boy on the chestnut stopped beside me, and the band was still playing and the sun still shining and it was one of those golden moments which you never forget.

Everything seemed possible now, jumping for England, riding at Madison Square Garden in New York, doing the American circuit, all the big shows in the United States, and Canada –

Toronto, Montreal. We were cantering round and I could see the Millers and Mum and Dad and Angus waiting outside, and nothing mattered but the feel of the turf beneath us and Phantom's effortless canter which felt as though it could last for ever, through countless rings, round Badminton, through days and days of hunting, for half my life at least.

ISBN 978-1-84135-820-8

PHANTOM HORSE

*I gazed in wonder at the view. Suddenly
I saw something moving below us. It was
a horse, riderless and alone. He moved
beautifully and with tremendous grace.
It was the wild palomino…*

When Jean's family moves to America,
her life is soon changed forever when she
meets the wild horse, Phantom.

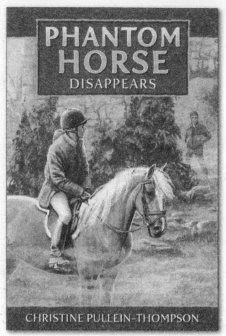

ISBN 978-1-84135-821-5

PHANTOM HORSE
DISAPPEARS

*"You're fools! Why couldn't
you leave things are they were?
Why did you come here?"*

When Jean and Angus discover the
terrible secret of Aunt Mary's house,
they are caught up in a dangerous plot
to kidnap their beloved Phantom.

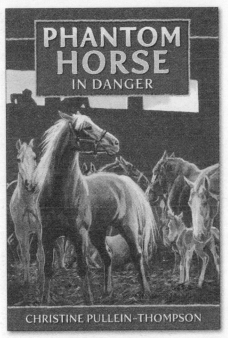

ISBN 978-1-84135-824-6

PHANTOM HORSE
IN DANGER

*I imagined Phantom twisting, kicking,
rearing, ropes round his quarters, a blindfold
over his eyes. The thought sent tears running
down my cheeks like rain.*

When their horses are in mortal danger,
Jean and Angus hatch a desperate plan
to save them. Will they be in time?

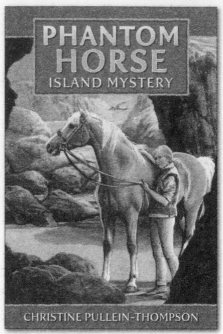

ISBN 978-1-84135-825-3

PHANTOM HORSE
ISLAND MYSTERY

The idyllic island where Jean takes
Phantom with her on holiday hides a
dangerous mystery. Why have most of
the inhabitants left, and why are horses
being secretly flown to the island?

When Jean is plunged into another
perilous adventure, can Phantom save her?

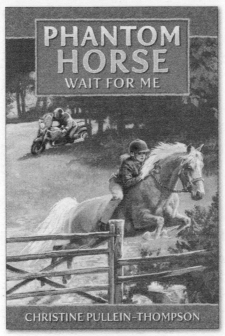

ISBN 978-1-84135-823-9

PHANTOM HORSE
WAIT FOR ME

*"Jean, darling, there's no point locking
yourself in your room. It won't bring
Phantom back..."*

When Phantom goes missing, little does
Jean suspect that her horse is the bait
in a plot to capture her. In a race for
their lives, will they escape in time?

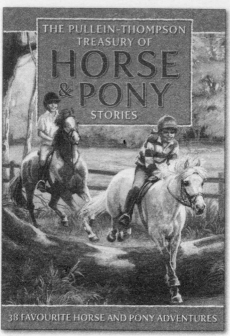

ISBN 978-1-84135-804-8

THE PULLEIN-THOMPSON
TREASURY OF
HORSE & PONY
STORIES

Packed with exciting adventures, this
bumper collection from the world's best-loved
horse storytellers will delight horse and pony
lovers everywhere.